HOSTAGE TOWER

They clustered around the set. Smith graciously allowed a commercial to wind up, then removed RTF from service and brought in the tower.

"It is now," he announced, "1 P.M. If the thirty million dollars I have requested is not in my hands within twelve hours, I and my associates will leave the tower—under the protection of our laser-guns. Shortly thereafter, four simultaneous explosions will reduce the Eiffel Tower to a scrap heap.

"I am sure," Smith continued, "that you would not wish that to happen. I am equally convinced that the president will not relish the thought that his mother will be in the tower when it goes up . . . "

Alistair MacLean's HOSTAGE TOWER

Written by John Denis

FAWCETT CREST • NEW YORK

A Fawcett Crest Book
Published by Ballantine Books

ISBN 0-449-20086-8

Manufactured in the United States of America

First published by Fontana Books 1980

First Ballantine Books Edition: May 1983

HOSTAGE TOWER

Alistair MacLean writes:

"Some time in 1977 two good friends of mine from the film world, Jerry Leider and Peter Snell, suggested that I should write some story outlines with a view to their being developed into a series of films.

"I duly prepared eight story outlines dealing with the activities of five members of a fictional group which I named 'The United Nations Anti-Crime Organization,' or, for short, 'UNACO.' *Hostage Tower* is the first of these stories to be filmed and it is the intention to produce films of the other stories in the future. Fontana recently suggested that I might like to write a novel based on the film. I declined because the timing didn't suit me—I was in the middle of completing my novel *Athabasca*. Fortunately Fontana was able to persuade John Denis to undertake the task—and you will soon discover what an excellent job he has made of it."

PROLOGUE

Lorenz van Beck had three hours to kill. For a man to whom killing came easily, it was time enough. But on that fine, pastel-golden Paris day, van Beck had nothing to kill but time.

Van Beck wandered through the leafy shades of the Ile Saint-Louis and basked in the dappled darts of sunlight that sought out his square, unsmiling face beneath its cap of spiked grey hair. He was hatless, and dressed in a dark suit of heavy broadcloth, his waistcoat buttoning high to bunch up the small-knotted, unimpressive tie. He looked, unsurprisingly, like a businessman.

With a muttered sigh, van Beck turned to business, choosing the Musée Rodin and the Musée de Cluny for modern art, porcelain, and glass. He noted recent additions, their placings and lighting, their security surveillance. He made jottings in a notebook: enter by this or that window; copy key to door 2, 9, 15; how big, how small, how friendly, the curator's guards; proximity to sewers, access roads; MO—bombs? Gas?

Occasionally he wrote down a name, one of a thousand —ten thousand—thieves, killers, weapons experts, explosives experts, biologists, hit men, stunt men, drivers, pimps . . . the freelance employees of Lorenz van Beck, international fence extraordinary. Against a particularly splendid loan collection of Venetian glass he set another name—a well-known name, titled, respected—a lady, you could say, of some quality. Not an employee, but a client.

3

Van Beck flipped back through the pages of the note-book to the diary section, and checked the client appointment he had made that day. He cast an eye at the gold watch chained to his waistcoat, sniffed the expensively musty air of the museum once again—what delicious odors wealth created!—and strolled to the car he had rented under a false name and driving license at the Gare d'Austerlitz. He retrieved a shabby leather case with an obstinate clasp from the front seat, locked the car, and abandoned it. It would later, he knew, be reported missing, but the matter did not greatly concern van Beck.

He made his way by taxi to another car rental office on the Boulevard Haussmann, where the pretty secretary recognized him as Marcel Louvain, and drove to Rambouillet by way of Versailles, stopping at the palace to sit in the lengthening garden shadows and eat warm bread and rough Ardennes pâté. The Rambouillet belltower boomed the first chime of six o'clock as Lorenz van Beck pushed open a creaking internal door and clumped into the darker silence of the church. . . .

The bell notes reverberated through the empty nave. Van Beck peered into the gloom, grunted, and plodded to the second in a group of confessional boxes set in the furthest shadowy corner. He pushed through the dingy red curtain, lowered his bulk on to the chair, cleared his throat, and sniffed in the direction of the confessional grille. A polite cough came from the scarcely discernible figure on the other side.

"Bless me, Father, for I have sinned," van Beck mumbled.

"In nomine Patris, Filii, et Spiritus Sanc—" the priest began, and was rudely interrupted by van Beck's derisive chuckle.

"This was your idea, Smith," he said, "but I'm a sensitive man, and play-acting becomes neither of us. Say what you have to say, and let me go."

"I rely, as always, van Beck," Smith returned in his dry, precise voice, "on your absolute discretion."

"And I on your consuming lust for making money illegally."

The vaguely outlined head nodded agreement. "Though you do me a small injustice," Smith said. "I am fascinated more by crime than by money, as you well know. For me, stealing ten dollars from the coffee fund in the desk of the secretary to the Director of Fort Knox is worth all the jackpots in Las Vegas . . . in the world.

"I have made crime my life's study, my life's work. It is the ultimate excitement, van Beck. No other physical experience can match it."

"Ja, ja," the Bavarian sighed, "so you have said, so you have said, Mister Smith. So you're different from me . . . huh? I can fence anything from the Mona Lisa to a uranium mine. I could find customers for the Taj Mahal or Beethoven's Tenth Symphony. I've even sold his own gold back to the Director of Fort Knox. But I'm a peasant. You're an artist. What do you want?"

"A team."

"To do what?"

"You know better than that, van Beck," Smith rapped.

"OK, OK." Van Beck was silent. "How many?"

"Three," Smith replied.

Van Beck wrote the figure in his dog-eared notebook. "Any preferences?" he inquired.

"None."

"So tell me."

Smith's urbane voice dropped to a sibilant hiss. "One— a weapons expert. The best. Tough . . . resourceful . . . professional." Van Beck's blunting pencil stump dug into the cheap paper.

"Two—a thief. Again, the best. I have to steal two and a half million rivets and somebody's mother." Smith giggled. "The best thief you know, van Beck. Daring, totally unafraid."

"What's the going rate for scrap iron and old ladies?" van Beck inquired.

"For this collection?" Smith said. "Could be thirty million."

"Rivets?"

"Dollars."

Van Beck whistled low, unmelodiously. "I can get a good team for a slice of that."

"Then do it," Smith whispered. "Do it."

"The third one?"

Smith hesitated. "Someone . . . inventive. Incredibly ingenious. Strong, and—again—afraid of nothing. Espe-cially heights."

Van Beck was thoughtful, rubbing his fleshy, prickly chin.

"That apply to the other two as well?" he queried, blandly.

"What?"

"The heights," the German replied, trying to fit rivets in the sky into a recognizable pattern.

Smith was quiet, dangerously quiet. At length he said, "Don't push me, van Beck. Do what you have to do, but don't try your luck too hard. It may not last."

Van Beck swallowed, and shuffled uncomfortably. "It will be as you say." He made to get up, but Smith's rasping command froze him.

"One more thing. There is a new gun, a laser gun, the Lap-Laser. The Americans have it for their army. I want some. The weapons man must get them. Agreed?"

"It'll cost."

"I'll pay."

"Sure," van Beck grunted. "You pay. I'll supply. That's business."

"Thank you." Smith relaxed back in his seat. "You may go. Contact me in the usual way. You have a month."

Van Beck nodded, making no reply. None was needed. He threw aside the curtain on its jangling brass rings, and strode out into the mellow light of evening. He drank white wine, marginally chilled, and cognac at the pavement table of a café, then rejoined his car and took the road to Chartres.

From the church porch, piercing eyes in a hooded face watched him.

Then the heavy door swung open once again, and a bent shabby little priest joined the homegoers and the evening walkers. He smiled benignly at an old woman dressed, like himself, in rusty black. He reached to pat the head of a passing boy, but missed.

CHAPTER ONE

*It was a sheltered place, twenty-eight miles west of Stutt-*gart: a plateau in wooded country screened from the road by trees, and hardly ever overflown. It made an ideal secret firing range. The US Army used the unfenced fields to test their newest toy, the General Electric Lap-Laser gun.

The US Army had four Lap-Lasers at Stuttgart. Not very many, they conceded, but still one-third of those known to exist. For the manufacturers had made only twelve so far, and they were as yet in the experimental stage. Since the Army chiefs were confident that neither General Electric's security nor their own had been breached, they took their time about putting the Lap-Laser through its paces. No one, after all, they reasoned, was going to steal it. . . .

On the day appointed by Smith for the theft of all four guns, a fine but drenching rain speckled the goggles of the Army's chief weapons instructor as he strained his eyes skywards to pick up the incoming helicopter. The fretful buzz of its motor sounded intermittently out of the heavy clouds. He chewed his gum viciously and spat, a not unaccomplished combined operation.

The helicopter was part of the daily Lap-Laser routine, bringing the precious guns from the big, closely guarded Stuttgart base to the range each morning, and taking them back again in the evening for safekeeping. The guns could not be tested at the base: they were too powerful, too unpredictable.

Apart from that, they needed an enormous power source,

7

and rather than transport huge and unwieldy banks of generators from place to place, the Army preferred the option of an isolated testing ground where they could install a small nuclear power plant.

The colonel glanced back over his shoulder at his sleekly sinister "babies," all four stripped and stacked away, ready to leave on the return trip to the base. He grinned and winked at his second-in-command at his side.

"They're really somethin' aren't they." It was a statement, not a question.

"Yeah," acknowledged the major, through a stubby cigar that rarely left his stained lips.

There were US Army generals, plenty of them, who would greet with genuinely blank astonishment any leading question about a laser gun, and the chief weapons instructor and his 2–IC basked in the realization that they were part of an impressively small band of experts. For example, if put to the trouble, which they rarely were, they would be able to explain that the Lap-Laser was made possible by advances not in ballistics or aerodynamics, but in the field of optics. That statement in itself was enough to confound most questioners.

The colonel grinned appreciatively at the final touch the laser gunners had insisted on adding to the already successful day's tests: at a range of a thousand meters they had drilled "USAAF" through a four-inch plate of sheet steel as cleanly as if it had been stenciled on cartridge paper.

The Lap-Laser's guidance system was similar to that of a conventional radar device, except that instead of using radio beams, it reflected beams of light when seeking its target. It could be sensitized to any target within its range, or any *kind* of target, because the mouse-ear detectors of the Lap-Laser, on either side of its firing mechanism, were tuned to distinguish the properties of a variety of different materials. They could run from a dozen different sorts of metal, to wood, brick, or the human body.

Once the target was located, the Lap-Laser sent out a concentrated ray of appallingly destructive force, which annihilated anything in its direct path.

Its other great advantage was speed. It is the practice in orthodox electronics to work down to a nano-second—one thousandth of a millionth of a second. If even greater speed is required, the only alternative carrier is light, which can be controlled to a pico-second, or micromicro-second—a millionth of a millionth fraction of time, of such minute duration as to be incomprehensible in human terms.

The Lap-Laser worked to pico-second tolerances, using a processor which General Electric built into the controlling computer specially for the job. To give the optical system the necessary speed to match the sophisticated laser gun, the processor employed minilasers no larger than a grain of salt.

Allied to a power source of massive concentration and force, the lasers combined to produce a weapon that was like a glimpse into a fearful future. Everything ultimately depended on the uses to which the Lap-Laser was put, and on the inviolable guarantee that it could never fall into the wrong hands.

Yet the hands of Mister Smith were among the dirtiest in creation.

And the instrument of his criminal ambition was at that moment speeding down an autobahn in a hired car to keep an appointment with the four deadliest "babies" of all time.

"AUSGANG-STUTTGART" the road sign read, and Michael Graham obediently urged the BMW into the stream that peeled off the motorway.

When the price was right, Graham was invariably obedient. Van Beck's price had been not only right, but generous. The unknown client, the German explained, was prepared to pay for excellence. And Mike Graham, van Beck had known, was awesome in his field of weapons and weapon systems. He had received the kind of training that only the US Army could supply, and had used a privileged position to enlarge his knowledge and raise his performance to a peak of unparalleled capability.

Smith had provided the means, through van Beck, to steal the Lap-Lasers, but the plan was Mike Graham's, and he turned it over in his mind for the thousandth time.

Using a laser-guided, tripod-mounted electronic surveillance device over a range of more than half a mile, Graham had bugged the US Army base guardroom to obtain the

weekly series of passwords that would gain him admittance
to the off-limits compound at the right time . . . when the
helicopter touched down on its run back from the firing
range.

Graham had also sounded out the other parts of the
base's territory which interested him: the officers' club; and
the living quarters for visiting top brass, whose faces would
not be known to the guards. He had selected and marked
his target officer, and now had a complete set of forged
papers in his new identity. He drove carefully along the
public road through the base, away from the off-limits
section, and pulled into a cul de sac not far from the
officers' quarters, located in a mini-apartment block.

Ten minutes later, a figure in the uniform of a general
of the United States Army strode the short distance from
the living quarters to the officers' club. He had a bundle
under his arm. He checked his wristwatch, peered up at
the sky, and made his way to a jeep parked at the rear of
the club.

The guard corporal dropped his girlie magazine and
jumped to his feet as the jeep screeched to a halt outside
the guardroom. He joined another soldier at the door, and
they peered out into the near-darkness. The harsh whirr
of the descending helicopter's engine sounded loudly in
their ears.

A man leapt lithely from the jeep, and the guardroom
lights winked on his general's stars. The corporal tightened
his grip on his M–1 carbine.

"Halt," he commanded. Graham did. "It's an emergency,
for Christ's sake Corporal," he shouted. "I'm in one hell of
a hurry."

"Advance and be recognized." Snorting with impatience,
Graham advanced. The GIs saw a man they did not know,
tall and bronzed, with brown hair and moustache, broad-
shouldered and thin-faced, looking at them from soft,
quick, intelligent eyes. He had a commanding, arrogant
manner. But then, the soldiers reasoned, generals usually
did.

"Hurry it up," Graham ordered. The banshee wail of the
chopper told him it would soon be settling on the launch-
pad in the compound beyond the guard block.

"Password," the corporal rapped.

"Don't play games with me," Graham snapped. "You first—that's the drill."

"Sleepy dog," the guard rejoined.

"Angle-iron," said Graham, handing over his papers.

The corporal recollected the name. "General Otis T. Brick." Visiting brass. Weapons expert. He snapped up a salute. "Yes*sir* General," he bellowed, while his subordinate pressed the button to raise the barrier to the compound.

Graham vaulted back into the jeep, gunned the motor to speed into the compound; and slowed to a halt in a spray of gravel near the launchpad. Three startled soldiers, waiting for the helicopter to come back from the range with the four crated laserguns on board, jumped like scalded tomcats when Graham screamed, "Get away from there—now!"

"Ten-shun!" barked the corporal in charge, and all three snapped into rigidity.

Graham saluted, and said, "Get your men away from this area. There's a leak in the nuclear generator shielding out at the range. The radioactivity could have spread to the guns, or even the helicopter. My orders are to take the chopper away."

"Who—who are you, s-sir," the corporal stammered. Graham had already raced back to the jeep and extricated the anti-radiation suit he had brought with him. Climbing into it, he shouted above the roar of the settling helicopter, "General Brick, Third Army Special Weapons Division. Now move it, soldier—move it!"

Graham reached back into the jeep and pulled out a geiger counter, and what looked like a steel briefcase. The helicopter's rotors were beating the air, and the pilot looked anxiously out at the charade on the tarmac. Graham ducked under the sweeping blades, and wrenched open the door.

"Out!" he ordered the pilot. "Radiation scare. You could have got a dose. The Emergency Med. Unit'll be here soon to check you over. I'll take the chopper away. Don't switch the motor off."

The pilot needed no second bidding. He scrambled out of the seat and dropped to the ground, almost colliding with Graham.

"Will you be all right, sir?" he screamed.

"The suit will protect me," Graham shouted. "I'll fly the chopper to the far end of the range and quarantine it. Look after your*self*, man."

The blare of a car horn from the direction of the guardroom drew the eyes of all four men on the ground away from the helicopter, where Graham was already revving the engine.

Two jeeps packed with men hurtled towards the launch-pad. A burst of machine-gun fire came from the leading vehicle. The three soldiers and the pilot scattered to hit the deck, and the jeeps pulled up short of a stack of gasoline cans a hundred yards from the chopper. Graham throttled viciously, and another spurt of tracer fire arced towards him.

Bullets pinged off the shell of the helicopter, and one tore a track across the shoulder of his anti-radiation suit, but he felt no pain. A third salvo stuttered out, and Graham, who had been about to take off, swore brutally. He snapped open the clasp of his briefcase and drew out a heavy, ugly Schmeisser machine-pistol.

He could barely see the two vehicles in the pool of blinding light, so he hit the easier target.

A vast swell of sound erupted as the gasoline cans exploded. The GIs were safe behind their jeeps, but there was now no possibility of stopping Graham.

Behind a concealing wall of smoke and flame, the helicopter rose into the air, taking the false general, and four crated but fully operative Lap-Laser guns away to do the bidding of Mister Smith.

The troops on the ground fired madly at the departing plane to ease their frustration, until the officer in charge resignedly flapped his hand in a gesture of dismissal.

"Who the hell was he, sir?" asked his sergeant.

"Christ knows," the captain returned wearily, "but he sure wasn't General Brick, because I've just been talking to General Brick in the officers' club. Somebody walked off with his dress uniform, and it wasn't his orderly, so it must've been that sonofabitch up there."

He tipped his peaked cap back on his head, put his hands on his hips, and whistled out a tight-lipped sigh. "Can you imagine the crap that's going to be flying around when the brass find out we've lost not just one of their favorite toys, but all four? Jeeze." He shook his head, almost admiringly. "You gotta hand it to that guy. He sure pulled a neat trick, whoever he is."

But the Army never did learn Graham's identity. The BMW was untraceable, and Graham had made no fingerprints. His abandoned clothing was unmarked, and in any case had been bought from a chain store. He might as well have been a ghost for all the clues he left. Or a spook.

He flew the helicopter eastwards for perhaps fifteen minutes on a prearranged flight path. Then he brought her in low and skimmed the treetops, his eyes combing the ground.

There it was. A winking light in a pool of blackness. He flashed his own landing lights, and three pairs of vehicle headlamps came on in answer.

Mike set the chopper down quickly and expertly, forming a square in the deserted field with the big, dark Citröen, the Volkswagen, and the tough little pickup truck that waited to greet him.

He ran to the larger car, and the driver's window slid noiselessly down. "You have them?" asked a man in the uniform of a chauffeur.

Mike said, "Yep."

"Excellent," the chauffeur returned briefly. He spoke guttural German. He reached over to the front passenger seat and handed Graham a loosely wrapped parcel and a briefcase of soft matte leather.

"Clothing, your size," he grunted. "In the valise—money, and the keys to the Volkswagen. Don't worry about the lasers. We'll load them into the truck. You'll be contacted for Phase Two. For now, disappear."

Graham opened the briefcase, and raised his eyebrows as he saw the fat bundles of small denomination US dollars. "Wow," he said. "Thanks." The chauffeur nodded.

Mike tried to peer beyond him to the man whom he could dimly see in the rear passenger seat, but a panel of tinted glass blocked his view. The windows were tinted, too. The man had not spoken a word, and sat hunched inside an enveloping overcoat, with a black Homburg pulled down over his brow.

"Thank you, too," Graham said, cheerily. The mystery man stayed silent and unmoving. Mike gave up the struggle and walked away, whistling.

The chauffeur turned and slid back the glass panel. "I'll transfer the guns and take the pickup to the warehouse, sir," he said, respectfully.

"Do that," Smith grunted. "I'll drive the Citröen and see you at the hotel. Don't make any mistakes. Graham didn't. He's good."

The chauffeur nodded. "And the helicopter?"

"Kill it," Smith ordered. "With Graham's uniform and anti-radiation suit in it."

Mike was a mile away when he heard the "crump" of the explosion, and saw in his rearview mirror the funeral pyre of the helicopter.

"You gotta hand it to that guy," he murmured, patting the briefcase on the seat beside him. "He sure pulls neat tricks, whoever he is."

CHAPTER
TWO

Weesperplein is not one of the great public squares of Amsterdam, like Sophiaplein, Rembrandtplein, or Dam Square itself, but its commercial importance is undeniable. That Friday evening, Weesperplein hummed with important traffic and prosperous, stolid people, as the armored security van nosed its way patiently along to come to a halt outside Number Four.

The uniformed, armed, and helmeted driver of the vehicle got out, and slammed the self-locking door. He walked around to the rear of the van, and tapped with his truncheon on the panel. Two men, also in uniform and wearing guns, alighted to stand by him.

The driver glanced at the clock above the heavy double-fronted entrance to Number Four, Weesperplein. The finely wrought gilt hands stood at four minutes to six. "Just in time," he remarked.

While the driver rang the bell, his colleagues manhandled a wooden crate on to the sidewalk by its carrying handles. The summons was answered by a man of medium height, balding, with mild grey eyes and a nervous manner. He nodded to the driver, who turned to his companions and sang out, "OK."

They heaved the crate up between them, and carried it inside. Then they returned and fetched from the van a precisely similar crate, and took that in, too. Both crates were heavy, and sealed.

When all three security guards came out, the nervous

man stood in the doorway, watching them depart. He shut the front door behind them, and checked that it was fully locked.

The driver glanced up again at the big clock. It gave the time as three minutes after six. "Home then," he said.

Number Four, Weesperplein, was an impressive, even beautiful, building, and the Gothic-script ornamental letters forming the frieze around the clock described in two succinct words what went on behind the imposing facade. The legend was "AMSTERDAM DIAMANTBEUR."

A brass plate on the wall carried a translation for the benefit of foreigners: "AMSTERDAM DIAMOND EXCHANGE."

Sabrina Carver made her first steal when she was seven.

She lived then—and for the next ten years—in her native town of Fort Dodge, Iowa, county seat of Webster County, as Sabrina learned at an early age, and immediately forgot.

It was also patiently explained to her that Fort Dodge had started life in 1850 as Fort Clarke, but the following year a pressing need arose to honor a certain Colonel Henry Dodge, and the name was changed. The fort was abandoned in 1853, so the tiny settlement, struggling to make ends meet in its uncompromising bed of river clay and gypsum, assumed the name.

"Good for Colonel Dodge," thought Sabrina, and immediately forgot him, too.

The Des Moines River, on which Fort Dodge stands, is still picturesque at that point, though it no longer rings to the cries of marauding Indians and defending settlers. It figured prominently in Sabrina Carver's young life, though, since it was the scene of that very first theft.

She was on a river trip with family and friends, and she calmly picked a tiny, silvery brooch off the coat of the lady who was sitting next to her, talking animatedly to Sabrina's own mother. The larceny passed unnoticed for half an hour, until Sabrina's mother spotted the brooch on her daughter's dress.

Though she was immediately forgiven by the gushing owner—"The poor, innocent little darling doesn't know, does she"—Sabrina made no fuss about giving the brooch back.

For this act of mature contrition, she received a quarter from the gushing lady, who petted her like a doll, for Sabrina had appealing dark eyes, long red-blond hair and a serious, saintly little face. As they were parting from her newfound friend, Sabrina stole the brooch again, and this time made sure her mother didn't see it.

She sold the bauble to the roughest boy in school for two bucks. It was a gross underpayment, for the brooch had three diamonds set into a silver clasp. But at the time, Sabrina failed to recognize them as diamonds. She thought they were glass.

She never made that mistake again.

From then on, Sabrina stole regularly to brighten her comfortable but tedious middle-class life. She had unearthed a professional fence by the time she was nine, and impressed him with her ability to deliver her dentist father's instruments, one at a time, over a space of three months. In that ongoing heist, she used a different modus operandi each time. The police were baffled.

All her education, her astonishing physical fitness, her command of sports and special skills, even her flowering beauty, were ruthlessly channeled into serving her overweening ambition to become one of the great thieves of all time. She chose new clothes, picture shows, books, lectures, holidays, only if they would widen her experience, or add to her prowess, or make the art of stealing easier for her.

Sabrina was, then, supremely dedicated. On her seventeenth birthday she left high school laden with prizes, and clutching a letter from the principal urging that she go on to Vassar, or at least Bryn Mawr, since she was the brightest student the school had ever known.

Her fence held sixty-seven thousand dollars for Sabrina in his own deposit account. By the end of the following week she had almost doubled her nest egg with the proceeds of a raid on a Des Moines hotel, which the police said could only have been committed by a small squad of acrobatic commandos.

Sabrina warmly thanked her friend the fence, withdrew every cent of the capital, and disclaimed the current interest. She used the money to set up in business for herself in New York, later establishing branch offices in Paris, Monte Carlo, Rome, and Gstaad.

She never once went back to Fort Dodge, Iowa, and had not made the slightest attempt to contact her parents.

Sabrina was a healthy girl and, at the age of twenty-five, almost indecently beautiful. Sex was easy to find, and she frequently found it.

At no time, however, did she allow any ulterior consideration to interefere with what, for Sabrina, was the ruling passion, the most intense pleasure, of her life. Not merely stealing, but stealing diamonds.

At stealing diamonds, Sabrina was indeed internationally acknowledged to be the very best.

There are probably more diamonds in Amsterdam than in any other single place in the world. Diamonds were first discovered in India, but the Dutch—who are inclined to treat anything of value with exaggerated respect—have been cutting and polishing them since the sixteenth century. At factories like Asscher's, eagle-eyed cutters peer at cleavage panes parallel to the octahedral faces, and divide the fabulous crystals with immense care, skill, and courage.

Asscher's it was who cleft the 2024-carat Cullinan Diamond. Joseph Asscher himself struck the master blow. Had he messed it up, his firm would doubtless have gone bankrupt, and the British Crown Jewels would have a lot of empty spaces in them.

Asscher's, and other manufacturing plants, are the places where the glamorous work of the diamond trade is done, but for dealing, the center is the Amsterdam Diamond Exchange. The Exchange, in fact, handles bullion of all kinds, which was why its security manager did not for a moment hesitate to grant a request from an important client, concerning not gems, but a consignment of gold ingots.

"I would not trouble you," the client, Kees van der Goes, had said, "except that I owe a favor to this friend of mine. He's got a big shipment of gold passing through Amsterdam at the weekend . . . at least, it was supposed to, but the outward journey to London has been delayed. He's asked me if you'd look after the crates for him until Monday morning. They'll reach you on Friday night."

Van der Goes, a well-known diamond and bullion dealer,

was a valued customer of the Exchange. The security manager, whose nervousness was endemic and practically boundless, agreed immediately.

"We'll keep the vaults open for the consignment," he promised, "though if you could possibly arrange for the crates to be delivered by six o'clock, then the time-lock can run its routine, you know."

Van der Goes said he would try, and the security men backed him to the hilt. They had all, however, reckoned without the dealer's pedantically fussy agent, who arrived at the Exchange shortly before the shipment, and insisted on examining at least part of the contents of both crates.

They had been carried through to the rear lobby, and there, the massive steel door to the vaults stood open, even though the electric wall clock showed seven minutes after six. The crates stood side by side on the metal floor. The fussy agent had just finished sealing one crate, and was about to open the other.

The nervous security manager's anxiety increased with each second that passed.

"Must you check the second crate?" he pleaded. "It's probably just the same as the first."

"I sincerely trust that it is," remarked the agent, "because it's supposed to be, after all, isn't it?"

"So?"

"But one must be positive, my dear fellow," protested the agent. "You would not wish me to do half my job, would you?"

"*My* job is to close the vault."

"And so you shall. All in good time."

The security manager shot the agent a glance of pure detestation, which was completely ignored. The agent unlocked the seals, and pried off the lid of the second crate. Like the first, it was filled to the brim with shiny gold ingots. As he had done before, however, the agent insisted in lifting up ingots from various places, to check the tier beneath. Finally satisfied, he lowered the lid, and laboriously replaced the clasps and seals.

Mopping his brow, the nervous one pushed home the vault door, spun the locking wheel, dialed the combination, and set the clock for the time-lock. The Amsterdam Exchange vaults would now remain shut, soundproof and airtight, until nine o'clock on the following Monday morning.

No human agency except a massive bomb could open the door from the outside.

And no way had yet been devised for performing the operation from the inside.

The stillness within the vault was almost palpable, the air heavy and hot. No sound came, and no living thing stirred.

So the shattering noise as the end panel of one of the crates was violently kicked out seemed all the more horrendous because of the oppressive silence.

Feet first, a dark figure wriggled into the total blackness of the vault. Despite the increasing warmth (which would eventually come under thermostatic control at 70 degrees Fahrenheit), the intruder shivered, for the place had about it the feel of the tomb.

The beam of a slim torch cut through the Stygian darkness, and illuminated the other crate. With tools from the air-conditioned "living space" in the first box, the burglar levered off the end panel of the second, and drew out more tools, plus battery lights, portable breathing apparatus, a radio, and a plentiful and varied supply of food and drink.

A battery light came on, and the dark form of the thief was revealed, clad from head to foot in the sinister all-black garb and hood of a Ninja Assassin.

Periodically, the hood was lifted to enable the intruder to breathe through a mask attached to an oxygen tank.

Finally, Sabrina Carver pulled the hood off altogether, and released her flowing hair. She switched on the radio, and settled down to a dinner of smoked salmon sandwiches and a bottle of excellent Pouilly Fouissé.

It was going to be a long wait until Monday morning, she thought, with only the theft of a small fortune in diamonds to while away the time.

The electric clock controlling the time-lock jumped from two minutes of nine to one minute. The security manager started in sympathy, despite the fact that his Monday morning routine of opening the vaults had not varied since he joined the staff of the Amsterdam Diamond Exchange twelve years before.

The machinery had merely gotten more sophisticated, and though the clock made no noise as it ticked off the minutes, the security manager, being nervous, acted as if the passage of the long hand was the crack of doom.

He was accompanied by the Deputy Director of the Exchange—again, as normal—and lurking discreetly behind them were two armed and uniformed guards. One kept a wary eye on van der Goes's fussy little agent.

Nine o'clock.

A white bulb over a switchbox next to the vault door blinked on. A plaque in the wall identified the box as the "Time Vault Release." A security guard reached out a long arm and, on the nod of the Deputy Director, pressed down a lever.

The security manager breathed a sigh of heartfelt relief, and stepped forward to turn the large combination dial, and spin the wheels in reverse direction.

The guards lifted their weapons and flanked the two executives.

With a solid metallic "clunk," the bolts inside the vault slid along their tracks, and the mighty door swung soundlessly out.

The security manager looked over his shoulder at his boss, smiling for the first time during the entire weekend.

The five men outside the vault barely had time to register the unbelievable scene . . . steel deposit boxes lying open, some scattered on the floor, clearly empty, alongside a trio of equally empty wine bottles.

Then the bizarre black hooded figure was on them.

The guards did little more than gape, because the intruder was completely past before they realized there had been anyone in the vault at all.

They were left with one scarcely possible, lunatic impression: the sound of whirring wheels.

It was only when the hooded figure had gone that one guard turned on his heel, fired off a departing shot, and shouted, "Roller skates! It had roller skates!"

In the outer lobby, secretaries and early arriving businessmen dived for safety as the apparition sped across the marble floor in long, crouching strides. Sabrina saw the far wall looming up, and made a dramatic power leg-over-leg turn.

The racing wheels of the skates fixed to her boots screeched jarringly on the marble as she clipped a corner and shot into a corridor.

The few girl clerks, more soigné secretaries, and portly office managers in her way scattered in horror and flattened themselves against walls or ducked into open doors to give her a clear passage.

Accelerating all the time, she pumped powerfully and unstoppably down the corridor, and from there to another, hunched forward in racing style, her arms swinging in surging rhythm, her eyes pools of brightness in the dark hood, a black knapsack clipped to her back.

Through a third corridor she rushed and a fourth, navigating a half-open glass door, and with more hair-raising right-angled turns, until she knew she was once more at the rear of the building.

It was an exhibition of breathtaking skill, streaking through knots of terrified people, skimming obstacles, trolleys, file-toting clerks, all the while gaining power and acceleration.

And finally, she was in a cul de sac.

She looked steadily ahead, gritting her teeth, bunching her muscles.

The passage ended not in a wall but in a floor-to-ceiling picture window. Sabrina careened towards it, went into an even lower crouch, let loose a yell of exultation, and sprang into the air.

She launched herself at the glass, booted feet and gloved fists leading, and pulped it to smithereens, bursting through into the cool air in a shower of splintered fragments.

Arms wheeling like a ski-jumper, she cleared the sidewalk and a disbelieving pedestrian. She landed fully balanced in the roadway and, without stopping, leaned into a turn and roared away down the slight gradient.

An area, no more than an alley, came up on her right, just where it should have been, just the way she had planned it.

She sped into it, dodging garbage cans, and reached a sheltered open space at the back of an off-center theater.

Behind her she heard the wailing sirens, and the shouts

of guards and police who were belatedly on her track. Sabrina spun to a stop and slipped off her skates, stowing them in the unsnapped knapsack. With a key from her belt she let herself into the almost deserted theater.

The people goggling at the unaccustomed activity in the quiet street took the dazzlingly lovely girl in the pantsuit for an actress, even if only because she had exited from a theater. She had a large tote bag slung over her shoulder, and she smiled winningly at the guards tearing past her.

Once in the Weesperplein, Sabrina caught a tram to the Rijksmuseum, spent half an hour there soaking up the Rembrandts, and walked through the pedestrian precinct to the Grand Hotel Krasnapolsky in Dam Square.

At the Amsterdam Diamond Exchange, the Deputy Director and the security manager were comparing notes with the police.

"I make it probably four hundred thousand dollars' worth in the unlocked boxes," the Deputy Director said, ruefully. "Thank God it was a slack weekend, and there wasn't more there."

"It was enough," the security manager intoned. "My, oh my, it was enough." He breathed out noisily, and shook his head in tragi-comic weariness. "Roller skates. I ask you— roller skates."

"What about my client's gold?" demanded the agent of Kees van der Goes.

"Nothing leaves here," interjected a stern-faced and harassed policeman. "Those are the orders."

"But the seals," the agent bleated, "they are untouched. The crates are as they were on Friday evening."

And they were. With the sole exception of the wine bottles—which she left on the floor out of sheer devilment —Sabrina had stowed everything carefully away in the crates, and repaired the end panels. With luck, they would pass scrutiny.

"So where, then," the policeman inquired icily, "did the guy in black spring from? Hey? And where did these damn bottles come from? Huh?"

For once, the agent had no ready answer.

CHAPTER
THREE

Enter the Black Spiderman.

There are times, even at night, when New York City—and particularly the canyons of the great avenues—seems to be made of glass.

Curtain walls of opaque smoothness, rising hundreds of feet into the air, suddenly, from different angles, come on like Christmas trees, and reflect the whole exotic panorama of skyscraper and strip joint, cathedral and cat-house.

Generally speaking, the bigger buildings are where the bigger people live, or work, or occasionally love, when they are not too preoccupied with living and working.

The big people like to have the trophies, the spoils of their rich and rewarding lives around them, if only to remind them how richly rewarded they are. Then they pay other, more talented, people to arrange the trophies in the most esthetically pleasing ways, and invite yet more people, who are less richly rewarded than they are, to come to their palaces and admire both them and their baubles.

The process serves two useful purposes: it teaches the visitors that the deadly sin of envy is a magnificent driving force; and it provides the means for the Pollocks, the Ming jars, and the Mayan masks to get the occasional dusting.

There is, though, one drawback: certain small-minded persons are importunate enough to wish to steal the spoils of the moguls. Thus, the trophies have to be guarded with such fanatical zeal that the pretty penthouse palaces become fortresses, or, worse, virtually prisons.

Happily, most of the lairs of the truly rich are nearly impregnable, and it must be a source of comfort to the criminal classes that these good citizens can sleep easily in their beds at night. So euphoric do the big people sometimes feel, that they will gladly lend out their treasures for public exhibition so that a great many people may see them, and slaver at the unostentatious plaque that makes it perfectly plain who is doing the lending.

If anything, these public displays are protected with even greater care and devotion than the private gloatings, for while the truly rich may not sincerely appreciate their treasures, they are the very devil when it comes to collecting insurance payoffs.

When the Black Spiderman gets bored with stealing from the millionaires' palaces, he will penetrate the public exhibition places with equally contemptuous ease.

On Manhattan's Fifth Avenue there are many glass mansions, as a latter-day prophet might put it. One stands in the block between Fifth and 58th and 59th. A poster tastefully mounted on an easel outside the building says: "LOAN EXHIBITION. THE T'ANG TREASURES. 38th FLOOR EXHIBITION HALL."

Much of the building is in darkness, but the lobby is well-lit, especially the elevators. Two men, both armed and in the livery of security guards, sit and talk and smoke. . . .

Up the steel-beamed glass wall C.W. crept. He was black-clad and black of skin, his bare toes as prehensile as his gloved hands. He did not have far to go. Twenty feet above him sat a window washer's gondola, attached to the vertical inset steel I-beam by a wheeled device.

C.W. reached it without breaking sweat, and climbed in. Slowly the gondola rose, almost to the peak of the building. C.W. scorned to count the floors: he would know the 38th when he reached it.

He looked down, and from side to side. The avenue, stretching out as far as he could see in one direction, was a ribbon of moving light-specks. The other way lay the dark menace of Central Park.

The 38th floor exhibition suite was not completely darkened. Though the exhibition had closed for the night, the choicest masterpieces of Chinese sculpture and metal work were permanently illuminated; some gaudily, where they needed it, others hardly touched by fingers of light that picked out salient features of wonderful artistry and delicacy.

C.W. peered through the window, and located the center-piece—a magnificent T'ang Dynasty Flying Horse. The Black Spiderman drew in his breath. The sculpture was almost too exquisite to handle. But it was his target. He had a commission to steal it, and in any case he would own it for a few brief, precious hours.

C.W. also noted the other form of illumination in the exhibition suite's main hall. Light-beams, laser-powered, crisscrossed each other like searchlights, seeking out and protecting the exhibits with a sureness that no human guard could match.

An intruder had merely to touch one of the glowing rays, and alarm bells rang out—not just in the exhibition suite and the lobby, and in the apartment of the building's head of security, but also at Manhattan Central and two other police precincts. The Flying Horse sat there, graceful and elegant, but dramatically charged with the suggestion of enormous, coiled power.

C.W. conceived the loony notion that all he had to do was whistle, and the horse would leap out of its prison into his arms. He tried it, and his warm breath blew back into his face from the window. He thought the horse winked, but he wasn't sure.

He sighed, and picked up from the floor of the gondola a large rubber suction cup. He clamped the cup to the window, and fixed the cord running from it to the stanchion of the I-beam. Then he took from his belt a diamond-tipped scalpel, and patiently traced a perfect circle around the perimeter of the cup.

He completed the maneuver several times, and replaced the scalpel. With the knuckles of both hands, he rapped the area of glass surrounding the suction cup, which was sitting on the skin of the window like a black carbuncle.

The ring of glass broke free, and C.W. carefully caught the suction cup and allowed it and its new glass cap to hang by the cord against the side of the building. He crawled through the circular hole, carefully avoiding a low, slanting light-beam, and stood in the exhibition hall getting his bear-

ings and adjusting his eyes and body to the changed lighting and temperature. He breathed in deeply and evenly,
and tensed his muscles for what, at best, could be only a
ten-second sprint to the horse, and back out to freedom.

For the Black Spiderman knew that he had not even the
remotest chance of stealing the horse and escaping undetected. That might be achieved by an army of electronic
experts and technicians, but C.W., as always, was one man,
alone. For him, it had to be the hard way.

His sole aids were his pantherish strength, his astonishing nerve, his natural ferocity, and his boundless contempt
for danger.

He had one other (for his chosen trade) admirable
quality: he was always self-contained, and rarely dealt in
violence. Violence against things, or obstacles—yes. Against
locks, doors, safes, security devices; but hardly ever
against people. C.W. valued people—even the truly rich—
almost as much as he valued the beautiful creations they
owned.

Drawing breath again, he let it out explosively, and
launched himself towards the center of the room.

When you are baptized Clarence Wilkins Whitlock and
your schoolfriends ask you which name you want them to
call you by and you say "Neither," then you might have
to fight to protect your nominal integrity. Clarence Wilkins
Whitlock reached this small crisis early on in life, and
established his right to be known simply as "C.W." over a
bloody, but gratifyingly brief, period in one of the less
favored districts of Tallahassee, Florida.

C.W. came from the wrong side of the tracks before the
tracks were even laid. He had an innate appreciation of
the natural beauty of that part of northern Florida where
Tallahassee sits on its perch high above the sea, in a nest
of rolling hills, lakes, and streams. When C.W. could get
away, this was where he liked to be, sitting by—or more
likely in—the little tumbling brooks, sunning himself on
the quiet uplands, and climbing the giant magnolia trees
and majestic oaks, hung in season with Spanish moss.

For C.W., home was always the haven, not of peace, but
of resentment; an island of poverty and bitterness in a sea
of plenty. Above all, it was the place where his racism

(and C.W. would accept that he qualified as a black racist) was nurtured. His youth had been the time of the awakening of black race consciousness, and that false dawn had a magnetic attraction for him. He did not actively loathe whites, but he was deeply afraid of them; and fear, he decided, was a more powerful emotion altogether than hate.

Only later, when he was beginning to establish himself to an unarguable degree, did C.W. discover that his fear of whites had turned to cautious regard, and then to grudging awareness, and finally to acceptance of them as a necessary aspect of *his* society. For without them, who would be the black's black? The Jew, perhaps? Polacks? Spics? Dagos? Wops?

Juvenile crime was a way of life for C.W. Whitlock before any alternative path had even been considered. And when, as he grew older, the question arose in his mind of a career, the choice—as it had been for Sabrina Carver— was easy.

For apart from a cool head crowning his lithe body, C.W. possessed one priceless accomplishment: he could climb anything, by day or night; any structure that he had ever been asked to climb, or been forced to. Some in his vicious circle of cronies dubbed him "Monkey," and quickly learned that C.W. did not take kindly to nicknames. Later he secretly reveled in being known to the American underworld as "The Black Spiderman": that, he felt, was a fitting tribute to an impressive talent.

But in the early days, he concentrated on going from strength to strength—or, more properly, from height to height. He devised ever more complex and daring pathways to robbery, and his gangster acquaintances were not surprised when he quickly outgrew his need for the basic talents of thuggery which were the limits of their collective repertoire.

He kept one friend, and occasional accomplice, Pawnee Michaels, a full-blooded black Red Indian, for God's sake. He went through Vietnam with Pawnee, and they traveled the road of crime together. But Pawnee was a liability, and knew it. Unadept and clumsy, he tried one day his own caper. C.W. watched him fall from the City Bank in Trenton, New Jersey, and turned away because there could be no percentage in claiming what was left of the poor, smashed body.

Since then, he had worked alone. Like Sabrina Carver, he migrated to New York, where the buildings were taller and more challenging. Again like her, he fenced through Lorenz van Beck. . . .

C.W. leapt the light-beams and glided between the statues, betraying no sign of his presence.

He landed on his toes by the central plinth, and froze, controlling his body, steeling his reactions. Then he plunged both hands into the cat's cradle of light, and seized the T'ang horse.

The infernal clanging of the alarms cut through the quiet of the building, like a bolt of lightning. The security chief jerked awake and smashed the clock from his bedside table. He swore and reached for the telephone.

The lobby guards raced efficiently through their drill, one heading for the elevator, and the other double-locking the front doors, then returning to bring down the three unused elevators. When they reached the ground floor, they would be immobilized.

He gazed hypnotically as the floor indicator of the occupied elevator raced up to thirty-eight. The phone rang. He palmed the receiver and said "Check. Check. Right." Then he slammed it back down, and crossed to where the three remaining elevators were settling, their doors opening in sequence.

The guard snapped off the operating switches to all three, and grinned. The bastard was trapped. Wherever he was hiding, he could not leave the building.

His security chief paused long enough to drag on his underpants, for he normally slept only in his gun. His apartment was immediately below the exhibition suite, and he made the stairwell in seven seconds.

There was no one on the stairs, either way. Nobody could have been quick enough to get clear, so the guy had to still be up there.

The security chief and the guard entered the suite simultaneously from different doors, and came within an ace of killing each other. But they were professionals, with quicksilver reactions.

The chief muttered "Shit!" when he saw the empty podium of the T'ang Flying Horse, and his guard shouted "There!" as he spotted the big hole in the window.

They sprinted over to it, stuck their heads out, and looked down. Down was where the thief must be, should have been . . . but wasn't. The security floodlights had been activated by the alarms, and the whole front of the building was clearly visible. They doubted whether even a fly could pass unnoticed on the glass palace.

So it must be up. And both men fired at the trundling gondola, which even now was within a few yards of the top.

"Get the roof!" the head of security yelled. "I'll send Tommy up, and make sure the police chopper's airborne." He leaned and fired again, and *saw* the bullets hit the metal frame, but could not be sure that they had penetrated.

C.W. flattened himself against the side of the gondola, and felt it judder to a halt as it reached the end of its track. He had been counting the bullets, and there was still the last of an estimated six to come. But he could delay his flight no longer.

He threw his body frantically upwards, and his questing fingers closed on the rough granite parapet which topped the building. Through the thin fabric of his gloves, he felt tiny chips of stone digging into his fingertips. His toes clamped on to the smooth surface of the facade like limpets. The last shot came, and ploughed into the granite an inch away from his left hand. Two fingernails split as he tensed his whole frame in mental and physical anguish.

The little cradle bucked under his feet. He gulped another lungful of air and made a last supreme effort to haul himself over the parapet. With a throat-wrenching grunt, he landed on the roof, and raced for the wooden shed housing the head of the ventilation shaft and air-conditioning central station. He knew it could be only a matter of seconds before the security guards got someone up there to seek him out, and he had much to do.

He tore open the parcel he had stowed there a week before, and quickly assembled the contraption that would take him to freedom. As he strapped on the harness, he permitted himself the briefest of sardonic grins. There was no earthly doubt that he would make it, given a lucky break, a few more seconds, now . . . given that, he was safe.

For C. W. Whitlock was one of the world's great experts at hang gliding.

He climbed onto the perch that was to be his launch-pad into thin air: the cover of the ventilation shaft. At that moment, the roof door burst open, and the security guard loosed off a volley of bullets. But he was a fraction of a second too late . . . C.W. had gone.

The Black Spiderman had never attempted hang gliding in a city before, and he would have preferred a less spectacular launch than throwing himself into a vertical dive down the wall of a skyscraper. But he had no choice.

It occurred to him with the stories flashing by and the wind tearing at his flailing body, that nobody else had ever tried hang gliding in Manhattan, either. Well, aficionados would soon know whether or not it worked.

He had planned the unorthodox technique of gathering tremendous speed for an all-out power glide rather than use the currents of warm air which rose from the city streets. It was to this specific end that he had chosen hang gliding for his exit: he dared not land in the streets, where he would be at the mercy of the traffic and the police. But if he could make the sanctuary of Central Park in one continuous leap. . . .

The slipstream was a dull roar in his ears, and the concrete and glass and marble veneer of the tower merged into a dark-grey blur as he plummeted towards the street. He tried pulling out of the dive, but he was going too fast, and the great, broad bulk of the neighboring skyscraper grew larger by the second.

He yanked the harness into the tightest turn that he dared, and almost wrenched his arms from their sockets. The soaring parallel streaks of light that traced the outline of another building suddenly swiveled through a right angle, and C.W.'s panic-stricken eyes gave his brain the mad message that New York had tilted on its side.

The skyscraper he was trying to avoid seemed for one appalling moment to be directly beneath his feet, so that he could land on it and walk down it like a fly down a post. Then he fought the wind, and straightened out, almost crying aloud his relief as the road slid away from his wing-tip, to resume its rightful place in the scheme of gravity.

He looked wildly about him, and saw that he was not

yet too low to catch a thermal current, if only he could reach one. Then, mercifully, a thermal found *him*. Almost immediately, but so imperceptibly that he failed to realize it, he started to rise.

He was now two floors higher than he had been, and still going up. At the moment, he was well out of range of the rooftop security men's guns in the exhibition building. But if he continued his ascent?

Yet the thermal zephyr was playful and, after lifting him fifty feet or so further, it shot him across the face of the neighboring skyscraper. He needed no prompting to steer around the corner and reach the end of the block. There, on the opposite side of 59th Street, were the welcoming trees of Central Park.

C.W. waved gleefully at a pair of lovers enjoying a session of palpitating sex in a fourteenth-floor apartment. They were so surprised at being spied on by a passing birdman that they pulled apart and fell off the bed. The girl, C.W. spotted, was a lulu. He made a mental note of the position of the apartment.

He rode the life-saving thermal across 59th, dropped lower in a controlled dive, and tree-hopped until he found an unobtrusive landing place. From there he linked with a pickup driver who had been waiting for him, concealed the hang glider and the Flying Horse under its false floor, and headed for home, scarcely noticing the minor irritation of the police roadblock at the corner of Fifth and 59th.

Lorenz van Beck stepped off the Rambouillet bus and walked across the square to a different café from the one he had patronized on his last visit. Today he wore a sports shirt in a violent check, a loosely belted open jacket, sunglasses and jeans. He downed a Dubonnet and made for the church.

The church clock welcomed him inside, and as he settled down in the confessional booth, he heard Smith rustling paper on the other side of the grille.

"Well?" Smith inquired.

"Bless me, Father, for I—"

"Cut it."

"I'm sorry," van Beck apologized, "last time I thought—"

"Never mind about last time. Now I'm in a hurry. Report."

Van Beck considered the situation, and how he might make best advantage of it. "Well . . ." he began, slowly. "I—uh—I take it you were satisfied with Mike Graham's performance? And, of course, you do have the Lap-Lasers —do you not?"

"We do," Smith agreed, "and I was. Very satisfied. I want him again, for the big one. Tell him. No details—not that you know the details, anyway—but make it clear he'll be very well paid."

"He already has been," van Beck returned.

"I know," said Smith, shortly. "When I buy, I buy only the best. My price for extreme skill is high."

"It shall be done," the German said. Then he fell silent again.

"Hurry it up," Smith snapped. "What of the others?"

"There are two whom I can recommend," van Beck continued, "because of their, as you so adroitly put it, extreme skills. The trouble is that they're loners. I just don't know how they'll react to working for you. They'll never have heard of you, of course, since you seem to adopt a different name and disguise for each little—ah—outing. Even *I* have no idea who you are, or which are the jobs that have been pulled by you, or at your orders."

"Good."

"For all I know, you could be my best friend."

"I'm not."

"Oh."

"However," Smith said, "if you are pursuing a devious route towards an increase in your fee, you need not strive so officiously. Ask, and you shall have it."

"Aaah," van Beck sighed. "In that case—there is a jewel thief, Sabrina Carver, and a cat-man, C. W. Whitlock, both in New York. I think they would suit you admirably."

"Sound them out," Smith ordered. "If they agree, tell both of them, and Graham, that they'll be getting further instructions very shortly. Plus money and plane tickets."

"Airline tickets to—?"

"Paris," Smith said. "From there, of course, it could be anywhere."

"As you say," the German agreed.

Smith rose to his feet. "This time," he smiled thinly, "you stay and I go."

"Unusual," van Beck replied, "but acceptable."

Smith walked quietly from the church. He was a taller, immaculately dressed, more confident priest than in his previous incarnation, and he held his manicured hands clasped in front of him, so that even eminently pattable children escaped his attentions.

And, still seated in the confessional box, Lorenz van Beck mused on rivets, heights, and Paris. This time, though, he got a definite picture forming, as if he had suddenly joined up a series of dots.

It was a very well-known shape indeed that sprang into his mind.

CHAPTER FOUR

There are probably fewer than a dozen nightclubs or discos throughout the civilized world where top-drawer international jet setters will admit to being seen. Il Gattopardo, in Rome, is one of them.

Dawn is a good time to be noticed at Il Gattopardo, though for the highest of swingers, an appearance at that hour will have been a reflex action, rather than a matter of calculation.

For Sabrina Carver, standing outside "The Leopard" waiting for her car, it was merely the end of a less than scintillating night. She distanced herself by about three yards from two quite beautiful young men, scions of top Roman families, close friends both of each other and of Sabrina, who were trying to settle a tactful argument as to which of them should go home with her.

The discussion did not interest Sabrina. She would have been tolerably happy with either, or neither.

Guilio and Roberto had reached a temporary accommodation, based on an apportionment of past rewards for Sabrina's favors, and future opportunities, when the parking attendant pulled up in Sabrina's Alfa Romeo. A portly, excitable little man with a waxed moustache and a too-large, braided cap, the attendant jumped out, held the door open for Sabrina, and bowed low over her generous tip. That way, he could also peer into her generous cleavage without seeming forward.

She settled herself into the driving seat, and the attendant

leaned in again, adopting the sort of confidential air at
which Italian operatic tenors excel. He handed her a small,
plain box, tied with pretty white ribbons.

"Someone left this for you, Signorina Carver," he whispered through an effluvium of garlic.

"Who?"

He shrugged extravagantly, using most of his upper body
and the ends of his moustache.

"Thank you," she said, and made with the lire again. The
attendant decided not to push his luck with the décolletage,
and backed away obsequiously. As Sabrina pulled apart
the ribbons, the entente of Guilio and Roberto fractured,
and they decided to settle the matter like gentlemen with
the toss of a coin.

Signorina Carver's educated fingers coped busily with the
wrapping. The attendant sighed, dramatically. "Bella, bellis-
sima," he murmured, and with good reason. She was classi-
cally, breath-catchingly lovely, with a cascade of hair
shaded now to russet-brown, falling on her bare shoulders,
framing a face that had more than once peered wistfully
out from the front covers of *Vogue* and *Woman's World*.
Gone was the saintliness of childhood, but not to give way
to artfulness or knowingness. Her brow was deep, her eyes
wide-spaced and round, her nose and mouth in exquisite
proportion, her chin cheekily dimpled.

How such a flower of Grecian beauty could ever have
been the product of that dour, grain-encrusted middle-
western state of Iowa had baffled Fort Dodge. Sabrina had
agreed, and settled the matter by leaving. Now her voice,
like her face and body, was international, and she kept
nothing of her childhood but her name, and her high regard for the stones which, as she could abundantly testify,
were indeed a girl's best friend.

Inside the box, in a bed of cotton and wrapped in tissue
paper, were five one-thousand US dollar bills, and a first-
class airline ticket to Paris. The flight was in three day's
time. There was no explanatory note.

She stared at the money and the ticket, blinked, and then
grinned as she noticed in the top left-hand corner of the
ticket cover, the scrawled initials "L. van B."

A coin was duly borrowed from the parking attendant,
and flipped by Roberto, as Sabrina throttled warningly and

released the hand brake. Guilio shouted "Ciao" while the coin was still in the air, hurdled over the back of the growling little car, and landed in the seat next to Sabrina. The Alfa screamed away and Guilio fastened his safety belt. He had never before ridden with Sabrina, but he was aware she had a reputation for a certain nonchalance at the wheel.

Upper Madison Avenue, New York City, like Fifth Avenue, is stacked with discreet, trendy little shops and boutiques catering to expensive and often esoteric tastes. There is also a sprinkling of way-out art galleries on Madison, to take advantage of the carriage trade's lust for artifacts that no one else possessed, nor indeed would wish to. "PRIMITIVES INC.," which the elegant and faultlessly dressed black man with the pencil-thin moustache was about to enter, was one such gallery.

"PRIMITIVES INC." dealt, as its name implied, in primitive art. This meant that it engaged agents, who hired other agents who, in turn, bribed African village headmen to lean on their tribes to produce badly carved, multi-hued bric-a-brac for half a bowl of gruel, which then sold on upper Madison Avenue for six hundred bucks apiece.

The receptionist sat at a gleaming steel and glass desk (Stockholm, c. 1978) amid a weird but well-arranged clutter of masks, assegais, and fertility symbols.

"Good morning, Mr. Whitlock," she smirked.

"And to you, Mary Lou," C.W. answered. Then he flashed her a brilliant smile and said, "Hey, that rhymes." Mary Lou grinned back. He was a dish, she decided; pity he was . . . well, you know, black. She tried to think of a suitable rhyme for "C.W.," but her intellectual equipment wasn't up to it.

"Anything doing, gorgeous?" C.W. inquired.

"It so happens," Mary Lou replied coyly, "that yes, there is."

C.W. was rapidly losing patience, but tried not to show it. The dumb white chicks, he mused, were even more of a pain in the ass than the smart ones, of whom there were not all that many.

"A message, perhaps?" he suggested.

"In back," she inclined her peroxided head. "You know."

"Indeedy I do," C.W. simpered. He rolled his eyes as he

passed her desk and crossed to the door leading to the lavish, semi-private display area behind the main gallery. Here the sculptures staring down at him from lucite shelves were, if even more wildly expensive, at least genuine and finely wrought. The semi-private nature of the rear gallery was required of the owners, because many of the costlier fertility symbols were all too explicitly fertile.

The gallery served (for a fee) as one of C.W.'s collection of New York dead-letter boxes, a facility that chimed in well with his tendency to divide his life into separate, equally secret, compartments. He had this in common with Sabrina Carver, too.

On a splendid oak refectory table sat a large, flat parcel. C.W. twisted the fastening string around his finger, and snapped the twine as if it were cotton. He shuffled aside the decorative wrapping paper, and looked with undisguised pleasure on a fresh wheel of his favorite French cheese, brie.

C.W. selected a Pathan ornamental dagger from the wall, and cut himself a generous slice. He bit into it. The rind was deliciously crisp, the cheese at a perfect creamy consistency. C.W. munched the remainder of the slice, then set the knife into the far edge of the wheel, and cut the entire cheese precisely in half.

He dipped the blade of the dagger into one segment, and traced a path along it. Puzzled, he repeated the process on the other crescent. The point of the knife encountered an obstruction. C.W. smiled, and hooked it out.

It was a small package, enclosed in rice paper. He scraped the rice paper off, and unfolded five one-thousand U.S. dollar bills, and a first-class airline ticket to Paris. The flight was in three days' time. There was no explanatory note.

He stared at the money and the ticket, blinked, and then grinned as he noticed in the top left-hand corner of the ticket cover, the scrawled initials "L. van B."

"Classy," C.W. said, admiringly. "Very classy." He walked out humming "The last time I saw Paris."

Bureaucracy thrives on paper. Paper demands circulation. In order to facilitate distribution bureaucrats love drawing up lists that squeeze as many people as possible on to them while, in order to save paper, confining them to a single sheet. Thus was born the acronym, an indispensable arm of bureaucracy.

The United Nations is bureaucracy run riot, and acronyms proliferate there like hamsters. Few of them are important. One, in a little-frequented part of the UN Building in New York, scarcely rates a second glance. The sign on the office door says: "UNACO." And below that: "Malcolm G. Philpott, Director." And underneath, "Sonya Kolchinsky, Assistant Director."

This acronym is misleadingly innocent, since "UNACO" stands for "United Nations Anti-Crime Organization," and it is very important indeed.

Sonya Kolchinsky picked up the ornate silver tray and carried it carefully across the room to Philpott's desk. Philpott's desk, like Philpott, was invariably tidy; there was plenty of space to set down the tray, which she did, again carefully. It bore a small espresso coffee machine, and cups and saucers in delicate china from a full service. Next to the silver sugarbowl and cream jug stood a cut-glass crystal decanter of brandy.

Sonya poured out a cup of coffee, and added a half-spoonful of demerara sugar. She stirred the brew and, without asking Philpott, slipped in a touch, measured almost in droplets, of Rémy Martin. She stirred the contents again, then topped it off with cream. Philpott, his eyes still glued to a file on his desk, raised the cup to his lips and sipped.

"Delicious," he remarked, absently.

"I know," she said.

He looked up at her, and grinned, a shade self-consciously. "Sorry," he muttered. "Miles away."

"You're forgiven." She inclined her head mockingly. She was of above average height, and statuesquely built. She had a round, slightly pug-nosed face, and lightish-brown hair, cut fairly short with a sweeping fringe, then layered back over her shapely head.

Sonya was in her early forties. Czech-born, but now a naturalized American. She was an expert linguist; she had a degree in molecular physics; and her IQ was a few points higher than the man whom she now faced. She had clear, grey eyes that twinkled at Malcolm Gregory Philpott, enjoying his temporary discomfiture.

She sat in a chair at an angle from the desk, and raised her eyebrows quizzically. "The list?" she inquired.

"By all means," Philpott replied. He placed a finger on his intercom buzzer, and a voice rasped, "Director?"

"The list."

"Sir."

In the large and roomy outer office, a young man in a sober suit, with a shaving rash and earnest glasses, picked up a message pad and started across the deep-piled carpet. He passed a wall-to-wall neon map of the world. In front of the map was a practically wall-to-wall inclined counter, a cross between a library reading-room desk and a ·Dickensian office-lectern.

Three technicians of differing nationalities sat at the counter in padded swivel chairs. Each wore a pilot-style headset with a tiny cantilevered microphone hovering a measured inch and a half from his mouth. The three were listening posts to the world. Occasionally they murmured greetings or commands in any one of more than thirty languages, ·and made notes on sheets of cartridge paper pinned to the counter. Every time a new call came in, a red light blinked on the map, indicating its origin.

An exact see-through miniature of the map, measuring no more than six by nine inches, rested on Philpott's uncluttered desk in a handsome frame. A mellow chime from an alarm system warned him when a new call came up, and the lighting pattern of the map was precisely duplicated, down to merest pinpoints from the most unlikely places.

The young man handed the pad to Sonya, who said, "Thank you, Basil," and began to study the neatly typed summary of the mid-morning traffic. . . .

Traffic in crime, which was the business of UNACO and its staff. Like Mister Smith, Philpott was fascinated by crime. He was, indeed, fascinated by Mister Smith; and there he had a decided advantage over Smith. For whereas Malcolm Philpott knew a great deal about Smith, and his many aliases and driving obsessions, Smith never even suspected the existence of Philpott or his department.

Philpott had himself suggested the formation of the top-secret group when he was a research professor in a New England university, heading a section sponsored partly by industry—it was highly technical and advanced research—and partly by the CIA, through the US Government. The government had fallen for the idea, and had even accepted Philpott's primary and absolute condition that the organization should come under the aegis of the United Nations, where its services would be placed at the disposal of all member states, and where its sources would not feel inhibited by the taint of American self-interest and militarism.

Philpott had not imagined for a second that the Nixon administration would not merely enthusiastically endorse the project, but also fund the donkey work of setting up the department. He was allowed to select all his staff and recruit agents, and had never for an instant regretted his first (and only) choice of assistant director.

Sonya Kolchinsky and Philpott shared the conviction that international crime, if properly organized, could threaten subversion and chaos on a scale to rival that of even the most belligerent Eastern Bloc state. They devoted (and sometimes risked) their lives and admittedly well-paid careers to fighting serious crime, and they had earned the respect and admiration of the vast majority of UN member nations, including some in the Eastern Bloc.

For UNACO would tackle crime anywhere, and for any reason, provided the threat to stability was critical, and that Philpott was sure the department was not being used as a pawn in a power game. He had known from the start that the Nixon Administration would try to subvert UNACO, by planting key personnel in the group. He had annulled that threat years ago and now, under a more malleable and far-sighted president, the department enjoyed the trust and support of the United States government and the unstinting cooperation of the CIA, INTERPOL and the FBI.

In fact, Philpott's personal relationship with the new president of the United States had opened doors to UNACO in America, and throughout the world, which had previously been closed to Philpott, whatever his credentials or reputation. It was a good time for UNACO. Malcolm G. Philpott was determined to keep it that way.

Easily the most persuasive explanation for his current

high standing was his astonishing success. And the most important influence on the UNACO hit rate was, without doubt, Philpott's ability to recruit international criminals to unmask international crime.

He logically put criminals into two principal categories: those who operated on their own account for their own benefit; and those others—such as terrorists of all kinds— whose activities were directed at governments, nations, and social systems.

There was a third kind—a rare breed of criminal dedicated to anarchy, wedded to the abstract concept of crime as a cleansing force; totally amoral and wanting in any respect for human life.

The second and third categories were Philpott's targets. He occasionally brought in governments to help his constant war against international terrorism. But the Napoleons of crime, the monsters, he reserved for himself, asking for help only when he needed it.

And he was winning his battles. For the criminals Philpott chose as *his* weapons were often the match for those he sought to destroy.

Which was why long since, he had recruited the master criminals Sabrina Carver and C. W. Whitlock to help him rid the world of Mister Smith.

Sonya scanned the message pad again, and said, "Right— here goes."

"The diamond trail's moving again, it seems. Reports indicate that an estimated two million in smuggled uncuts leaked out to Capetown yesterday. Courier unknown. Action?"

"Is someone tracking the haul?" Philpott asked.

"We are."

"OK. Code Blue. Give it to INTERPOL, Amsterdam."

Sonya wrote in a neat hand in the margin opposite the coded entry. Then she resumed, "Czechoslovakia forensic has identified the poison in the Branski assassination."

Philpott grinned. "With a little help from you, I imagine. Yes, good. Make it a Yellow, and send the thing to our own lab for a fast report."

· Sonya made the notation. "Gold?" she said. Philpott nodded. "Heavy unloading by the Bombay Irregulars."

Philpott winced and sighed. "That's a Green."

"Sure?"

"Sure."

"And now," Sonya announced portentously, having kept the best news for last, "we have a Smith affirmative out of Rome."

Philpott sat back in his chair and slapped the gleaming desk with the palm of his hand. "Great!" he enthused. "Sabrina hooked him. Great!"

"With a little help from us and van Beck," Sonya protested.

"We didn't help with that Diamond Exchange robbery," Philpott said. "We can't do that sort of thing, after all. The Dutch would never forgive us. Neither would INTERPOL."

"We can keep our fingers crossed that nothing goes wrong, though, can't we?" Sonya asked.

"And we do," Philpott agreed. "Mind you, it's not really necessary with Sabrina. I reckon she could have done it on her head, let alone on roller skates."

Sonya half rose from her chair. "Would you like to speak to her?"

"Yes," Philpott replied, "I'd love to—but not just yet." Sonya seated herself again and looked at him inquiringly.

"Well," Philpott explained, "if Smith's bitten with Sabrina, then he ought to be doing the same for C.W. Has he called?"

Sonya was about to say "No," when the chime pealed, and the map on Philpott's desk glowed with a fresh pinpoint of light. "Ha," he said. "New York. Now, I wonder who this could be." He directed that the call should be put straight through to him.

C.W. reported briefly and succinctly. "Excellent," beamed Philpott. "Three days, eh? Not much time. We'll be there with you, though, and then we'll find out what it is. At the moment, it's enough to know that Smith's behind it, so it'll be pretty damned serious and spectacular."

Philpott hung up and regarded Sonya steadily. "Now," he mused, slowly. "I wonder what, and precisely where. . . ."

"Paris, I suppose," Sonya put in. "Why send them tickets to Paris if the action's somewhere else."

"Ye-e-s," Philpott conceded. "And it's true that van

Beck's come up with some absolutely crazy idea that just doesn't seem to make sense. All the same . . ."

"What idea?" she demanded sharply. Philpott did not normally keep secrets from her, and she had right of access to most UNACO information—unless Philpott considered it might be dangerous for her to know.

He grinned, sheepishly. "D'you mind if I don't tell you at the moment?" he said. "I want to consider it a little further. It's—way out. And it may mean nothing. Or everything."

Sonya relaxed. "Sure," she agreed. She furrowed her brow in thought, bit her lower lip, and ventured, "So it's just the laser guns we're not fully up to date with yet?"

Philpott nodded. He stroked the left-hand edge of the bridge of his nose—a favorite trick when he was thinking too hard. His face was lined, but still handsome. He was perhaps ten years older than Sonya, and his hair, though plentiful, was grey and slightly tousled. He had a strong, pointed jaw and skin stretched tautly over high cheekbones. He was lean and fit and, for an ex-academic, scrupulously well-dressed. Sonya Kolchinsky was in love with him, and he knew it.

"The lasers," he said. "The lasers—yes. Who took them? And why? And for whom?" He was silent for a while, and Sonya did not disturb his train of thought. Philpott tapped his fingers unevenly on the desk. "For Smith, I imagine," he argued with himself, "and more than likely for this job. As to who took them—it could be anyone." He shrugged, and nodded at the file in front of him. "We both believe it's a weapons man, and they're all in here—all the top suspects. Ex-army, ex-CIA, grudgeholders, suspected agents . . . It's just a question of picking the right one. It's a pity," he reflected, "that van Beck couldn't help Smith find a weapons man. Then we'd have all three in our pocket."

Mike Graham sauntered out of the Munich bierkeller and crossed to the busy square fronting the magnificent cathedral. Anywhere in central Munich was not too far from The Four Seasons Hotel, which was one of the great hotels of Europe, and which at present numbered Graham among its guests.

He walked through the square, and took a short cut to

the fruit and vegetable market. Between a pair of enticing vegetable stalls sat an old woman next to a small, trestle-mounted cart. The cart held packeted wienerschnitzel, and chestnuts popped on a free-standing brazier.

Graham was wearing jeans, and a leather flight-jacket which had seen better days. A white kerchief fluttered at his throat, and he sported an American Legion badge over the top left-hand pocket of the jacket.

"Guten morgen," he said to the woman. Her sharp eyes took in the kerchief, the badge, and the face above it.

"Good morning," she replied, in heavily accented English. "Would you like some chestnuts for a not-too-warm day?"

Mike nodded, and said, "Ja, bitte." The elderly woman took a paper bag from the cart, and picked freshly roasted nuts from the coals with a pair of tongs. "They are hot," she warned, "very hot. Mind your fingers."

Graham assured her he would. He gingerly extracted one, cracked and peeled it, and popped it into his mouth. It was delicious. "Auf wiedersehen," he said. "Goodbye," she replied.

He strolled back down the street, and took a seat at a pavement café for coffee and schnapps. He emptied the chestnuts out on the table to cool. The packet was at the bottom of the bag.

He opened it and, shielding the contents with his other hand, unrolled five one thousand U.S. dollar bills, and a first-class airline ticket to Paris. The flight was in three days' time. There was no explanatory note.

Graham opened the folded airline ticket. In the top left-hand corner was a poorly executed sketch of a Lap-Laser, accompanied by a terse message: "Now I want you to use them." The message was unsigned. Mike drained his schnapps and ordered a refill.

Guilio was sitting as though bolted into the seat of the Alfa Romeo. They were well south of Rome now, and he had not even bothered to ask Sabrina where they were going. He just fervently wished he was somewhere else.

He had brought it on himself. Guilio freely acknowledged, when he unbuckled his seat belt. Sabrina had been driving with great restraint—for her—when Guilio had sensed that the time was right for one arm to slip around her shoulders, while the other hand skated over, then settled on her knee. He could not have been more wrong.

She stepped fiercely on the gas pedal, and Guilio's head shot forward and rapped smartly on the fascia. The Alfa's engine shrieked, and Guilio dimly saw a road sign saying "Roma 170"—pointing in the opposite direction. He resigned himself to an early grave, and hoped his mother and numerous sisters would cry at his funeral.

Sabrina reached a corner, made a racing change, and screamed round the bend, kicking dirt on what seemed to Guilio to be only one wheel. It was a short road, and another bend was coming up, for they had long since abandoned the autostrada for more taxing sport. Sabrina double-clutched down through the gears, and drifted into a toe-to-heel braking power turn before gearing back up for the straight. The motor protested, but obeyed her feet and her tensed arms.

Guilio's handsome face shaded to chalk-white, his eyes glazed over, and his bowels turned suddenly to water. He could see a narrow, hump-backed bridge looming up, and he quickly recited what he was certain would be his terminal prayer.

Sabrina turned to bestow a ravishing smile on him, taking her eyes completely off the road while, at the same time, pressing the accelerator pedal down into the floor. Guilio gripped the Alfa's crash-bar so hard that his knuckles matched the white of his face. He closed his eyes and let out a scream of undiluted horror.

Sabrina gunned the motor, and with a roar of triumph the little car sailed off the bridge and launched itself into the air. It settled on the road again just in time to get into a power drift along another sharp bend. Sabrina was laughing with sheer delight, when a different sound intruded above the squeal of the tires and the gruff whine of the engine. It was an insistent and penetrating electronic bleep. As she pulled out of a turn, Sabrina took her foot off the gas and let the car ease down to a modest twenty mph. Guiding the wheel expertly with one hand, she reached under the dashboard and pulled out a radiotelephone mike.

Sabrina spoke into the microphone, "Pronto."

Sonya's voice came over the line: "Is the pasta al dente?"

"Not yet," Sabrina said. Then, "Hang on a sec, will you?"

She steered the Alfa Romeo to a halt on the grassy shoulder of the road. Guilio slumped forward on the crash-bar, sobbing piteous thanks to as many saints as he could remember. Sabrina opened the dashboard locker and pushed a code key into the scrambler box fitted there. "Scrambled on 8-2-Baker," she said into the mike. "Do you read me?"

"I do indeed, my dear," Philpott replied. "Are you alone?"

"Why hello, Mr. Philpott," Sabrina said, "what a pleasure to hear from you. No, I'm not exactly alone, but he doesn't understand a word of English. In fact, at the moment he doesn't seem to understand much of anything." Guilio turned his dazed eyes on her, and leaned back in the seat with his mouth drooping open.

Philpott brought her up to date with the news that C.W. would be joining her on the Smith caper. "Oh, great," she crowed. "Give him a hug for me, and tell him I'll keep him out of trouble."

"And you look after yourself too, young lady," Philpott ordered with mock severity. "I want you looking your best on Friday, because Sonya and I will be there as well."

"Why you sure enough bet I will, Mistah Philpott, Suh," Sabrina replied. "So for now—ciao, baby."

"Sabrina!" Philpott commanded, "don't go, I haven't finished. Those diamonds. You'll have to give them back, you know. I can't permit members of my organization to commit real crimes while you're in my service. You see my position, don't you?"

"What?" Sabrina yelled. "Hello! Hello, New York, hello? Are you still there, Mr. Philpott? Something just terrible seems to be happening to my equipment, you know? Ah well, whatever it was you said, I'm sure it wasn't all that important. Bye now," she chirped and broke the link.

"Wouldn't you say so, Guilio?" she inquired of her cataleptic passenger.

"Glug," said Guilio. In Italian.

Philpott chuckled, and flipped a key up on his communications console. "That girl," he said, "will—"

"—keep you young," Sonya supplied.

Philpott winked. "No, you do that," he whispered. Basil reentered the room.

"And call the Secretary General, Mrs. Kolchinsky," Phlipott ordered, brusquely, "and see if he can get us a Red priority from the French Government."

"Yes, sir," Sonya said, head buried in message pad.

"And get us two seats on the fast one to Paris Friday morning."

"Right away, Mr. Philpott."

Basil placed a folder on the desk, and made to leave the room. Philpott lowered his voice conspiratorially and said to Sonya, "And make sure we have our usual room at the Ritz."

"Of course," Sonya whispered, and turned to go.

At the doorway, where they met, Basil winked at her.

CHAPTER
FIVE

Steam rose from the softly swirling waters of the Jacuzzi.
Smith rode the tingling currents, and thoughtfully patted
a whirlpool of bubbles which erupted to the surface, spoil-
ing the sculptured undulations. The vortex subsided, and
eddied away.

Smith measured the length of his body on the buoyant
waters, and lazily paddled afloat. He heard the clickety-
clack of footsteps on the tiles, and smiled a foxy smile. He
sniffed and smelled Calèche or Cabochard. It didn't matter
which. The body that wore it was well enough known to
him.

A robed arm stretched out, the long slim fingers curled
around the stem of a Venetian air-drop glass. He let the
amber liquid stay, admiring the delicate curve of the menis-
cus. Seconds, a minute, two minutes, passed. Life, and
time, were trapped in a cryogenic matrix, the surface of
the liqueur still in contrast to the restless pond of the
Jacuzzi.

Smith was stoned out of his head.

His eyes drifted together, swiveled apart; then he lay
back and breathed a tiny, muted sigh. He focused on a
blob of condensation trickling down the tiled wall, a dribble
that transmuted into a cataract, tumbling and foaming until
its maddened breakers overwhelmed the room, the gardens,
the grounds, the château, all of Orléans, all of France, all
that lay beyond.

He hiccuped, and nodded. The glass tipped obediently

towards his mouth, and the sparkling fluid slipped down his throat.

Smith was still stoned out of his mind.

He spluttered, and the hand bearing the amazingly proportioned glass withdrew. Leah sat back on her heels, and regarded him with affectionate amusement.

Smith said, "I have been thinking, Leah."

"Yes, you have, haven't you." She spoke English with him, but in tones overlaid with her native Vienna.

"Why is it, Leah," he murmured scarcely audibly, "that with all this money I have . . . this adorable château, and the other places . . . the yachts, the ranch, the island . . . the pictures, the sculpture, the jewelry collection, the books and autograph scores . . . not to mention you and my other —little friends . . . everything . . . everything . . . I have everything, Leah . . more than any man has a right to dream of owning . . . well, almost . . . I don't have the Great Wall of China—but I could get it."

"Yes, you could, my darling." She was blonde and Nordic, not too big, but lushly voluptuous; her eyes were greeny-blue, her face and body enticingly rounded, all dips and curves, valleys and delicately swelling mounds. Smith owned her.

"Why is it, then, that I am cursed with this disease, addiction . . . pestilence of crime? It's not even aesthetic. It's . . . positively plebeian."

Leah lifted well-shaped eyebrows and smiled indulgently. "Plebeian?" she queried. "The theft of the Black Goyas from the Prado? The substitution of Troy in the Prix de L'Arc de Triomphe so that even his owner didn't spot it? The Liz Taylor ring, straight off her bath tray with a magnetized fish-hook? The Inca sunburst smuggled out in a pizza? Plebeian?"

Smith's mouth pursed into a lazy smirk. "Mmm," he purred. "You're right, of course. They said the Bloemfontein Krugerrands were untouchable, too, didn't they? And the Tutankhamen Exhibition that left London laced with pinchbeck. And what about that exploding ping-pong ball of Chairman Mao's?"

Leah giggled. "And the Fabergé eggs!" Smith laughed. "That's right," he said. "Melted, didn't they? Into rather good chocolate, actually."

Leah stood up. Smith nodded. With a casual oscillation of her body, she shrugged off the robe, and stood naked before him. Her breasts were upturned and expectant. She parted her legs. His eyes traveled down her inviting form to the vee of her thighs. He nodded again, and she stepped into the Jacuzzi.

"No," she breathed, "not plebeian, my sweet. You are endlessly inventive, and for you life, without crime, would be death. You *have* to have it. And besides, if you didn't, you'd be so bored . . . and boring."

Smith wasn't absolutely sure he caught what she had said, and granted her the benefit of the doubt. Boring he was not. He stretched out an encircling arm, and Leah floated within it. She moaned softly as their bodies fused with practiced ease.

The château stood in its own grounds, stretching several hundred acres, south of Orléans. Its parkland had been laid out and maintained in a state of unnatural and almost geometric perfection.

There were horses in the stable that Smith seldom rode. There were reaches of the garden he had never visited; rooms of the château he had never entered. The château was a possession, and Smith was plagued by possessions.

As he himself had said, he lacked for nothing. He was going to make a cool thirty million dollars from his current enterprise, yet money was the last thing he wanted. True, it brought him power . . . but who needed power? Smith, who changed his appearance and lifestyle so often that he had genuinely forgotten what he looked like as a young man, required only sufficient power and influence for the next crime—and the next—and the next.

If people got in the way, or governments, or nations . . . then they must be removed. Smith cared nothing for people, for humanity as such; and even less for nations. Where had he been born? Paraguay, was it? Or Samoa? Could have been. Iceland, even. In which language had he first spoken the faltering words of infancy? Did it matter? All tongues were his now; he had but to choose. All peoples were his; he was a citizen of the world, with a hundred names and faces. He demanded nothing from life, and he surely gave nothing to it.

Smith turned, and felt for Leah, knowing she would be there. Someone was always there. It did not matter who it was.

A helicopter descended to the lawns outside the château, and a young man, tall, dark and muscular, with a wicked scar giving an evil cast to an otherwise pleasant face, crossed to the front step. His name was Claude Légère, and Smith owned him, too.

Smith and Leah lay locked together as Claude knocked at the Jacuzzi room door, and Smith said, "Come in."

Claude stopped short when he saw the couple and stammered, "Forgive me. I thought you were alone."

Smith withdrew from her, and regarded Claude mildly. "You know I'm never alone," he said. "Is everything all right? It must be, or you would not be here. You would not dare to be here."

"Of course everything is going well," Claude protested. "How could it be otherwise?"

"True," Smith conceded. He fondled Leah again, but under the surface of the water. Somehow, it seemed to Claude even more obscene.

"I—I am going to the airport now," he ventured. "I'll pick up our new recruits and bring them here."

Smith turned to him. "Not straight here, obviously," he warned. "You'll follow the procedure we agreed."

"Yes, yes," Claude assured him hastily. "Please don't worry, Mister Smith. Every possible care will be taken to safeguard yourself, your identity, and this place. It will be done as you said. When they arrive, they will not have the slightest idea where they are, or how far they have traveled, or even whether it's still the same day."

"Good, good," Smith sighed. "Everything on schedule. That's how I like it. That's how it should be, Claude."

"It is," Claude insisted.

Smith turned in the water, and stretched out his legs. Leah followed his movements, then drifted to the edge of the Jacuzzi, hoisted herself up, and sat dripping on the edge.

Smith grinned at Claude. "Would you like to join us?" he offered.

Claude controlled his breathing with difficulty, and tore his eyes away from Leah.

"Another day, perhaps," he said, "when I am less occupied. But thank you for asking."

"Don't mention it," Smith said. "You're welcome, any time."

The clouds grudgingly parted, and Sonya, in a window seat of the Concorde, looked down on the futuristic disc of Charles de Gaulle Airport, twelve miles northeast of central Paris on the broad, flat plain of Ile de France.

A stewardess arrived to collect their empty glasses, still awash with the remains of the ice, and Sonya's with a twist of lemon. Another stewardess came with a note.

"It was radioed through from the Élysée Palace," she whispered. "You must be very important."

"I am," Sonya whispered back.

"She means *I* am," Philpott grunted, slumping further down in his seat.

"Would you sit up, then, please, Mr. VIP?" the stewardess requested, "since we shall shortly be landing at Charles de Gaulle Airport."

"If we don't," Philpott acknowledged, "it will indeed have been a wasted journey." The girl grinned and wiggled off.

Sonya opened the slip of paper. "From Giscard," she said. "You've got your Red priority."

Philpott sat bolt upright at this, then folded his arms behind his head, and leaned back in his seat with a complacent smirk on his face, like a cat that's just cornered the cream market.

The Concorde dipped into its final descent, leveled out, and caressed the runway, its long, pointed nose skimming the tarmac. Philpott—who had a horror of VIP suites—took Sonya through the Concorde gate into one of the seven satellite buildings of Number One Terminal, in the slipstream of executives and pop stars who make up the normal daily cargo of the flagships of Air France.

They joined the "travelator" crush, riding inside totally enclosed glass tubes, to the first nest of three concentric levels in the terminal dish: the Transfer Level, a mezzanine through which all arriving and departing passengers must pass. Philpott kept his eyes skinned, but could see no one he recognized.

They went through passport and Customs controls, and boarded the next travelator up to the Arrival Level—another sub-division into three concentric areas: the inner baggage hall, topped by a ring of Customs control filters, and finally an outer gallery leading to buses, taxis, and the parking lot.

They collected their cases, and waited in the outer gallery —for there were many things due to happen shortly in Charles de Gaulle Airport that interested Philpott.

Two passengers they already knew about—Sabrina and C.W., who would arrive on different flights, but near enough at the same time. And Philpott was sure they would be met. He had to know who was meeting them.

But it was the third potential traveler that concerned him most. For if Sabrina and C.W. had been summoned to France to serve Mister Smith that day, then so, too, he reasoned, would the laser-gun thief be similarly called.

Malcolm Philpott was most particularly anxious to see the laser-gun thief. He could be the key to Smith's destruction or to the defeat of UNACO.

A Pan-Am Boeing 747 followed the Concorde down, and C.W. took the fantastic trip, wary all the time, through the Transfer Level to the Arrival Level. Philpott, seated at a restaurant table on level two, spotted him, but looked quickly away.

Half an hour passed, and then the Munich flight turned up, delayed by some minor industrial action. Michael Graham lounged against a pillar next to the baggage carousel that claimed to be able to produce his case. He spotted it, and made a quick lunge for it. As he did so, the public address system rasped his name. "Mr. Graham, Mr. Michael Graham, passenger from Munich. Will Mr. Michael Graham please go to the lost luggage office on level one."

Graham threaded his way through the green Customs channel, and got directions to level one. There was a small queue at the lost luggage office, and he joined it. He was in no hurry. He identified himself when his turn came, and the clerk placed a small pocket radio on the counter.

"Yours, I believe?" the girl asked.

Mike studied the radio. Nothing happened by chance in the dangerous game he was playing, he reasoned, so he said, "Yes, it is. Where on earth did you find it?"

The girl laughed. "*Not* on earth, as it happens. You left it on the plane, and the stewardess remembered seeing you with it. She knew your name, so she brought it to us."

"Well, thank her for me," Mike said.

"I did," the girl replied. "We're only glad you didn't lose it for good."

"Yeah," Mike said. "Me too."

A stewardess caught up with Sabrina Carver on the travelator. "You dropped this as you were leaving the Rome plane, Signorina," she puffed. "A little radio—see?"

"Hey, so I did," Sabrina returned. "How stupid of me. Thank you very much indeed."

"You're welcome."

C.W., to whom impatience had more than once been a virtue, got tired of waiting for a contact. He stalked up to the information desk in the Arrival Level, and demanded if there had been a message left for him.

"Not a message, sir," the official said, "but apparently you were supposed to collect this."

He handed C.W. the radio, and C.W. said, "Jeeze, so I had to. Guess I forgot all about it. Thanks." He looped the radio on to his right shoulder by its carrying strap.

Sonic bleeps were keyed simultaneously to all three radios at intervals of two seconds until their owners had the sense to switch on the receivers.

"Good," said Claude's voice. "You should all be receiving me now. If you are, acknowledge."

"Loud and clear," said Graham. "Uh-huh," from C.W., and "Roger, or whatever," from Sabrina.

"Right," Claude went on, "now please listen carefully. I want you to ride the travelators until I tell you to stop. You will receive instructions during the course of the trip. The passenger from Rome will start from level one, the passenger from New York from level two, and the passenger from Munich from level three. When you arrive at a disembarkation point, you will simply take the next available travelator, in the reverse direction. Understood?"

Affirmative. "Munich?" Sabrina thought wildly. "Who

the hell's from Munich?" C.W. chewed over the unexpected gobbet of information. "Three of us, huh? So?" he mused.

Philpott and Sonya had split up as a security precaution, and Philpott was playing the part of a tired man squatting on a case in the corner of the ground level central arrival area. He looked at his watch occasionally, heaved dramatic sighs, and morosely chewed a chocolate bar. He watched in bafflement as Sabrina started her weird odyssey in the glass tubes, and sat bolt upright when he saw the object she held clamped to her ear. A radio, was it?

"Damn, damn, damn," Philpott gritted. So there would be no personal contact. Instructions by remote control. "Clever bastards."

Though the ruse did give him one slight edge: he could keep Sabrina and C.W., once located, in plain sight as they rode the steeply ramped, space-age tubes, crisscrossing each other at dramatic angles.

And all he'd have to do was find another traveler with a radio jammed to his ear, and he had the Third Man. The laser-gun thief.

He scanned the travelators. They were crowded, and it was difficult work. There? No . . . there! No . . . just scratching. Ah—C.W. And Sabrina getting off. And back on yet another travelator ending up somewhere else, he supposed . . . but no Third Man. Where is the bastard, where is he? And what the hell are my two people listening to so intently?

Claude whispered, "Stand by for a message from your employer. Again, listen well."

Claude—who was in a telephone booth nearer to Sonya Kolchinsky at that moment than either of them realized—held a small but efficient tape recorder next to the microphone of the two-way radio, and clicked on a switch.

Philpott saw C.W. take out a cigarette lighter and palm it in the hand holding the radio. "Good boy," Philpott breathed, "Good boy."

Smith's voice carried to the three on the ramps, caught in the tubes like goldfish in elongated bowls.

"Welcome to Paris," he said. C.W. cocked his ear at the cold, emotionless, neutral tones. Familiar? No, he decided.

"You will call me Mister Smith," the voice said. It was

an unarguable statement. "I am now going to give you the terms of my offer. There is no negotiation. You may accept the offer, or reject it. If you do not wish to cooperate, you will find a return ticket to the place from which you came, waiting for you at the 'reserved' section of the ticket desk on the ground level.

"No immediate sanction will be taken against you if you refuse my offer, but I feel I should warn you that you will never again work for me, or for any organization that I control; and you will discover that my operation is worldwide. If you are prepared to take that chance, then feel free to say 'No.' I do not, however, recommend it."

C.W. remained impassive, but a frisson of alarm crossed Sabrina's face. Of the three listeners, she alone had heard the name before in a criminal connection. And Sabrina wanted above all to go on working. Mike Graham merely grinned; he took neither the name nor the threat seriously.

Philpott still frantically combed the travelators for the laser-gun thief, and Graham just as obstinately stayed shielded by an enormous African in flowing chieftain's robes, who seemed to be riding the ramps out of sheer exuberance. Wherever Mike went, the Zulu went; Graham actually began at one point to suspect the giant African, but the expression on his face was so fatuously innocent that Mike correctly diagnosed him as a travelator freak. Some people felt like that about subway escalators, he recalled.

Smith continued, his tone still expressionless. "If you accept my terms you will, from that moment, be incommunicado. Further, you will be required to obey me, or my authorized representatives, as soldiers obey their commanding officers. Any breach of discipline will be treated with the utmost severity. The punishment for treachery is death." C.W.'s eyebrows lifted, and Sabrina's mouth set in a hard line. Philpott kept his eyes on her. She was more responsive than the taciturn black.

"However," Smith went on, "I do not intend serious injury to anyone during this operation, least of all to one of you three. On the other hand, should it be necessary, I may require you to carry out an order to kill. It is doubtful, but it could happen, so I have made it a condition of your acceptance."

This time it was Mike Graham who registered surprise, although of the two killers in the group (C.W.'s victims had been in the line of duty in Vietnam) Graham was the more accomplished assassin.

"In exchange for your acceptance of these terms," Smith said after a slight pause, "I shall pay you the sum of one million dollars—each. You will receive this fee whether or not the operation is successful. You have ten seconds in which to consider your reply."

The three moving faces on the travelators registered emotions from delight to incredulity. For C.W. and Sabrina there was, in any case, no choice; their agreement would be automatic. And from Graham, there was never an instant's hesitation. It was an awful lot of money.

Claude snapped off the tape recorder, and said into the two-way radio, "Mister Smith will have your answers—now."

There was a heartbeat's delay, then C.W. drawled, "Tell him, yes." Sabrina said, "I'm in." And from Mike Graham, "Sure. Why not?" Claude seemed satisfied, and gave all three fresh instructions.

Philpott saw that C.W. and Sabrina were now heading by a "down" travelator to the ground floor level, and he guessed correctly that the electronic conference was over. That meant that his chance of spotting the laser thief had gone. He signaled to Sonya, and moved out into the center of the busy concourse.

Sonya marched furiously up to Philpott and gave him a good old-fashioned dressing-down in tart, idiomatic French. Where had he been? she demanded. Why had he left her? What the hell did he think he was doing?

Philpott replied in kind, in fact going several better, and Sonya turned majestically on her heel to leave him standing there, throwing one final insult to his manhood over her shoulder. It was then that she collided with a well-dressed young black man, who was about to light a cigarette with an expensive-looking lighter.

The man lost his balance, and dropped his lighter to the ground. He stooped, a little slowly, to retrieve it. Sonya mouthed a confused apology and joined him, getting to the lighter fractionally before C.W. She handed him the lighter, smiled, and he walked away.

Sonya then walked back to Philpott, apparently contrite, even affectionate, and lay her head on his shoulder. "Did you make the switch?" he whispered. "Of course," she replied, pressing C.W.'s lighter into his hand.

Philpott slung his arm around Sonya's shoulders, picked up his bag, started to maneuver her towards a SORTIE sign—and suddenly stopped dead in his tracks. He pushed Sonya behind the corner of the information desk, and turned towards her, so that his face was hidden from the main body of travelers.

"What's wrong?" she hissed.

"There's a man walking towards the exits," Philpott whispered, urgently, "tall, brown hair, no hat, leather flight jacket, dark jeans. See him?" She nodded.

"The one with the radio slung over his shoulder?" she said.

"Radio?" Philpott echoed. "Fantastic! I didn't spot that. Then it must be him."

"Him?" she queried. "The laser-gun thief?"

"Yes. I know him—or at least I know of him. And I've met him a couple of times. I can't understand why he wasn't in my file . . . he fits the bill so perfectly. His name's Michael Graham, and he's ex-CIA."

"Ex?"

Philpott nodded. "Yes. Three years ago he had a break-down of sorts. I don't know what caused it, but he upped and left the company. Since then, I believe, he's been thought of as a renegade. Certainly he's violent and unstable. He could be extremely dangerous."

"Is he good?" Sonya asked, trying not to look too closely at the retreating figure.

"The best," Philpott answered. "Grade 'A' weapons and weapons systems. Fabulous operator. Knows lasers inside out. In fact—" his brow furrowed, "I've got an idea. . . ."

"What?" she pressed.

"I've got an idea," Philpott said slowly, "that the reason why he isn't in my file must be that someone took him out, to throw me off the track, because he would surely have been included in any list of potential laser-gunners. It can only mean Smith has a CIA plant."

Sonya gasped, "That could be critical."

Philpott said, "It could. Also—there's . . . something else

about Graham that's at the back of my mind, but what it
is I can't for the life of me think at the moment. I know
it's important, though. . . . Ah well," he shrugged, "no
doubt it'll come back. Anyway, first things first: we've got
to follow them and find out what they're up to."

They had lost Graham, but C.W. hung back on the pre-
text of buying a carton of Lucky Strike, and made it easy
for them to trail him. He increased his speed, curious to
meet at last the man from Munich, the third conspirator in
the Smith caper, whose special skills neither he nor Sabrina
had been able to guess.

C.W., who knew the location of his next destination
from previous visits to Charles de Gaulle Airport, got to
the helipad a minute before Sabrina. Claude was there, and
identified himself as the radio voice. They would meet
Smith later, he promised.

Sabrina arrived, looking breathless and devastating, and
C.W. shook hands with her courteously when they were
introduced by Claude. "How nice to be working with such
a beautiful lady," he gushed, but managed to make it
sound sincere. They accompanied Claude into the helicopter standing on the launchpad.

Philpott and Sonya, hanging back at a safe distance, and
peering around the corner of a cargo hangar, stared at each
other in consternation. "That," Philpott remarked heavily,
"has done it. Smith has been too crafty for us again. Almost
as if he knows every move we're making, and is laughing
up his sleeve when we get hung up at each turn."

"You're right," Sonya agreed. "How the hell can we follow them in a helicopter?"

"We can't. It's my fault. Bad planning. I should have
had something ready in case of an eventuality like this."

"With a Red priority," Sonya pointed out, "you still
could." Philpott shook his head. "Good idea," he said, "but
it's too late. They'll be off immediately. No point in their
hanging around. The best I can do is get their flight plan,
if they've filed one, which I doubt. In any case, what's to
make them stick to it?"

"What could they do?" Sonya asked. "They'd have to
make the best of it," Philpott answered. "Sabrina's good,
C.W.'s very good, in a corner like this. It's up to them now.

They'll get in touch if they can. I only hope that bastard doesn't foul things up for them."

She followed the direction of his outstretched finger. Mike Graham, who'd been reoriented by a helpful airport employee, hurried to join the aircraft. The door swung open to admit him, the motor exploded into life, and the giant rotors started to turn.

Sabrina and C.W. were on their own. . . .

Graham counted six people in the large chopper. He knew none of them, from the brief glances he'd had at their faces. One was a doctor, white-coated, and with a stethoscope hanging around his neck. Four of the others lay on stretcher bunks lining the sides of the aircraft. Mike reasoned that the only other man standing must be the one in charge; he nodded at Claude and said, "Mike Graham." Claude shook his hand.

Sabrina, who had been studying him covertly from her stretcher, turned her head quickly and faced the helicopter's curving internal wall. First the face, she thought . . . now the name! She *knew* him. And she knew what he was—or what he had once been. For what she had heard about him since they last met had not been good news.

"Meet the others later," Claude said to Graham. Mike noted that one of his colleagues was a sassy-looking black; another a woman; the third a seemingly short, beefy, bull-necked man; and the last one an Asian of some kind. The doctor was—a doctor, and Claude, the scar-faced man, was clearly French. When Claude motioned him to a bunk, he sank on to it without argument.

He closed his eyes, since everyone else seemed to have, but a sinister hissing sound made his eyelids spring open. The doctor was bending over the bulky thug, holding an anesthetic to his face.

Mike guessed it was Smith's idea of total security, and made no objection when the doctor crossed to his stretcher, hovered low, and administered the gas. In fact, he welcomed it. The doctor had bad breath.

Philpott and Sonya listened in stony silence to the recording C.W. had made of Smith's tape on his cigarette lighter

—a bugging device of great sophistication and accuracy, invented by UNACO, and plugged now into the stereo system of the chauffeured limousine placed at their disposal by the French Government.

"... *if you accept my terms you will, from that moment, be incommunicado* ... *punishment for treachery is death* ... *carry out an order to kill* ... *one million dollars— each.*"

Sonya whistled, and Philpott grimaced. "Thank God," he said, "that I can rely on the loyalty of C.W. and Sabrina, because that's a great deal of temptation. But they're too well-trained to fall for it ... I hope."

The radiotelephone in the car sounded a warning bleep. Sonya picked it up—and as she did so, Philpott lifted his hand and smacked it down on his thigh. "That's it!" he shouted. "I've got it! Training! Of course. That's where it was."

Sonya was speaking urgently into the mouthpiece, and making notes on her ubiquitous message pad. She finished, cradled the receiver, tore the top sheet of paper off the block, and handed it to Philpott. He studied it intently, and nodded, grimly.

"It's him all right," Sonya said. "Dismissed from the service January 14, 1977, after a severe breakdown. Erratic behavior ever since. And that"—her lacquered fingernail tapped the page—"is what you couldn't remember, isn't it, Malcolm?"

"I just did," Philpott replied, closing his eyes and letting his head slump back on the expensive upholstery. The tinted-window car pulled up outside The Ritz.

"He was their best weapons expert, and it was only natural that he should turn up occasionally at training courses for CIA and invited outside personnel, as guest lecturer. It's just our luck—or Smith's—that Graham should have been specialist demonstrator on the CIA course we fixed up for Sabrina just after she joined us."

Sonya reached for his hand. "A teacher doesn't always remember every student he's ever lectured to," she said softly.

Philpott opened his eyes, and flashed her a grateful smile. "Honey," he said, "If you were a man, would you remember Sabrina Carver?"

Sonya blinked. "I see what you mean."

Philpott opened his eyes again, and sank back into the cushions. "What I mean is precisely this," he murmured. "If Mike Graham *does* remember her—as I believe he will —he will almost certainly denounce her as a spook plant to Smith."

"And?" Sonya said, not wanting to hear the answer.

"And Smith will kill her. Don't you recall what he said? *'The punishment for treachery is death.'*"

CHAPTER SIX

*Claude stood at the doctor's shoulder as he leaned solici-*tously over Sabrina's inert form. The doctor peeled back a dark-fringed eyelid, and exposed the milky-blue white of her eye and the tremendously dilated pupil.

"Is she OK?" Claude wondered, anxiously.

The doctor rounded on him. "Of course she is," he snapped, "why shouldn't she be?" Claude began, "Well—" but the peppery little medico bridled and started a tirade of medical inconsequence. Claude held up his hands, and backed off.

"It's all right, I'm not criticizing you," he assured the doctor. "It's just that . . . well, Mister Smith said . . . you know—"

"I am perfectly aware," the doctor announced pompously, "what Mister Smith said. Let me remind you that I am the medical authority here, and while these people are in my care, and provided ignorant outsiders do not attempt to interfere, no harm will come to them. Of course, if you want me to tell Mister Smith that you made a thorough nuisance of yourself and got under my feet—" he let the proposal hang in the air.

"No, no," Claude protested, the panic rising in his throat. "You're in charge. I just wanted to be absolutely certain that nothing was going—sort of—wrong."

"Wrong?" the doctor thundered. "This young lady's pulse, blood pressure, respiration, heart and lungs, and for all I know her pelvic girdle and her big toe, are in excellent condition. She is as fit as a Stradivarius, and has a better color than you do. I am about to examine my other patients —if you would be so kind as to get out of my way."

Claude slid aside, and took himself forward to plague the pilot. He looked moodily out of the window, but even the mellow beauty of a perfect early autumn day failed to cheer him. The helicopter chased and followed its own shadow across a succession of emerald green fields, great pastures of corn and barley, tidy little farms, and ruminative Charolais cows. They were barely an hour out of Paris, but Claude, a blinkered metropolitan Parisian, was already homesick for the city. He mistrusted the countryside, and everyone in it.

He peered more closely at the incoming horizon. The château grew larger in the vision frame.

"Piss off, Claude, there's a good chap," the pilot said. "You make me nervous."

Claude threw up his hands, and returned to the main cabin, where the doctor was completing the examination of his last patient.

"Are they clean, doc?" Claude inquired, respectfully. All five unconscious passengers had their clothing loosened or removed. The doctor sighed, but good-humoredly. "They have no obvious diseases, they do not take drugs intravenously, and, with varying degrees of proficiency, they have washed today. Also, which is what I imagine you are seeking to establish, none has a concealed weapon. Right?"

"Right," said Claude, flashing him a conciliatory grin. He knelt on an unoccupied bunk, and looked out of a side porthole. The château was close now, and Claude was at last moved, if not to wonder, then at least to admiration.

It was one of the thirty or so great châteaux of the Loire Valley, which span in age a period of more than five hundreds years. It lacked, perhaps, the glamour and renown of the fabulous Blois trio of Chambord, Chaumont, and Cheverny, or the royal palace of Blois itself. Nor was it a massive fortified keep like Sully-sur-Loire or Château Angers, with its seventeen round towers.

It was not garishly splendid, like Jacques Coeur's renaissance palace at Bourges, nor conspicuously gracious, like Talleyrand's Château Valençay. But Mister Smith's Château

Clérignault was secluded, immensely comfortable and stylish, and probably housed more art treasures than most of the other castles combined. It was indecently sybaritic, and truly beautiful.

Its roof was crowned by a great bronze eagle, surmounting a forest of spires, bell turrets (in working order), gilded weathervanes, and tall, noble chimneys. Three fantastically contrived towers formed a triangle at either end, and bisected the rear stabled quadrangles. Narrow dormers near the eaves gave way to windows of majestic proportions moving further down the ivy-mantled front elevation. Steps, lined with statues, rose from the lawns to the great double doors, which were flanked by naked caryatids supporting a huge crenellated shell.

Outside, the gardens rivaled the landscape park in glory and inventiveness, from the high, mirrored surface of the water garden down to the ornamental garden and the Italian garden, and the vegetable and herb gardens surrounded by box trees. Hornbeams and fountains stood where the myriad paths crossed, and there were trysting bowers everywhere, which in past years had shivered the sighs of adulterous love. Smith preferred his Jacuzzi or his king-sized round bed with wall-to-wall mirrors.

"Give them their wake-up juice, will you, please?" Claude requested. The doctor set to work cheerfully with a hypodermic.

Ten minutes later, the helicopter banked over the magnificent park, and settled decorously on the lawn immediately in front of Smith's castle.

Leah waited for the rotors to stop. The door opened for her, and she climbed gracefully enough into the cabin. Smith's new recruits had by then recovered consciousness, and Sabrina was leaning forward at the window marveling at the splendor of the château.

She turned around when Leah spoke. "Welcome to Château Clérignault," the Austrian woman said. "My name is Leah Fischer, and I am Mister Smith's personal assistant. I hope you've had a pleasant journey, and are suffering no unsettling aftereffects from the anesthetic. Do you have any immediate questions?"

"I do," said Graham. He held up a finger and rubbed it

along one of the windows. A colorless grease mark was deposited on the glass. "Why was I fingerprinted when I was knocked out?" he demanded.

"You all were," Leah remarked, pleasantly. "Clearly we have to confirm your identities against our files. When that's been done, both you and we can sleep more easily in the knowledge that we're among friends."

Mike relaxed, looked across at Sabrina, and grinned. She smiled back, trying to disguise the rising tension and uneasiness she felt.

Never by any word or sign or hint had Mike Graham betrayed that he even recognized her, let alone knew her for what she was. Was he merely biding his time for a dramatic denouncement? she wondered. Did he want to betray her to Smith in person, perhaps to earn part of her million-dollar share as well as his own? Or could it be that he had failed to spot her, even though she instantly knew him? Sabrina thought not—she had no false illusions about herself; she was convinced that to a man like Graham, she was nothing if not memorable.

Her grin became rather fixed, and as she looked away she saw that his still appeared genuine, unforced, and guileless. It was the kind of smile a man might try on a pretty girl whom he didn't know at all . . . or no one he remembered all too well.

"Follow me, please," Claude instructed them. C.W., nearest the door, jumped out first, and turned to help Sabrina. She held his arm for balance, and he guided her down.

"My, but you're polite, fella," Graham sneered. C.W. turned, and met Graham's cold, disdainful eyes with his own challenging gaze. Mike grinned, and said, "D'you mind moving now—unless you're going to help me down too?" C.W. spun on his heel, and stalked away.

"Watch yourself, Graham," cautioned Leah. "Mister Smith doesn't like friction, and he may decide that Whitlock or Sabrina are more important to the operation than you are. Now that you're committed, that would not be pleasant for you. Nobody leaves a Smith project once begun, unless it's in a box."

"Well, Mister Smith may be due for a surprise," Graham

said. "Meanwhile, it's kind of you to mention it. I'm grateful."

"I'm so glad," said Leah, levelly.

Leah, clad in a rough-spun one-piece jumpsuit, but still managing to look decorative, led the way—not into the imposing entrance of Château Clérignault, but to the rear of the house, skirting the kitchen gardens. They came to a stable yard, where half a dozen men, dressed as Leah was, sat hunched around a weapons demonstrator. A large target in the form of a fresco of four running figures spanned the far end of the yard.

Leah held up a hand, and the file halted. The demonstrator swiveled the powerful heavy-caliber machine gun on its tripod to face the target, a hundred yards away. She shouted a command, and the figures began to move: down until they almost disappeared, darting up again, lurching from side to side, all at bewildering speed.

Casually, with crisp, economic bursts of fire, the gunman cut them to pieces, one by one. As far as Graham could tell, not a single bullet was wasted. He concentrated on just one cut-out dummy—a sideways crouching commando. The head went first; then a projecting arm was slashed off; the torso was neatly bisected; and finally each leg was separated at the kneecap. It was an impressive performance, and Mike got the feeling it had been laid on specifically for his benefit.

"Are these guys part of our operation?" C.W. inquired. "Not necessarily," Leah replied. "Mister Smith has many little—exercises—in training in various parts of the world, under different field commanders. Yours, however, will have his individual attention."

"We're honored," Graham ventured. Leah ignored him, and then led the way to the stable block. They passed through a tunnel into another, smaller yard, where a massive black stallion was coupling with a whinnying mare. Further bursts of gunfire, and the brutal lunging of the impatient horse lent the graciously proportioned buildings an unwanted air of animal savagery.

Claude nervously gave the rutting stallion a wide berth, and passed with Leah into the long, pine-paneled gun room. There, a cold table had been laid out, with chilled manzanilla sherry and aperitif wines flanking a quadrille of lobsters, crabs, and choice hams.

"Mister Smith thought you might prefer to lunch here, and get to know each other properly, since you're going to be thrown together quite a lot in the days to come. So . . . enjoy each other's company. Mike, Sabrina, and C.W.— you haven't in any case met Pei and Tote properly.

"Pei's from—Indonesia, is it?"—the happy little Asian nodded, and grinned even more spectacularly—"and Tote here is Finnish. We've never been able to spell his name, let alone pronounce it, but he's quite happy to be known as Tote." The immensely broad and squat gorilla looked as though happiness was a condition entirely foreign to him, but he twisted his lips into what he clearly imagined to be a pleasant expression, though the effect on the three Americans lay somewhere between a snarl and a snake bite. Pei, however, seemed to approve, and slapped Tote smartly on the back.

"Shall we be seeing Mister Smith soon?" Sabrina asked. She was curious to get her first sight of the man who, she had inferred from snatches of conversation with Philpott, was capable of causing untold harm to UNACO—and the world.

"No," Leah said. "In fact, you won't see him today at all. You'll meet him tomorrow morning, though. When we've finished lunch, I'll take you to your rooms, and you can settle in. Later, we'll go on a quick tour of the château and the training grounds. May I caution you once more that you are not in any way to seek to communicate with, shall we say, the outside world. The telephones here are not for your use. Members of the staff will not carry messages for you. Even an attempt to make contact with anyone, no matter whom, will be construed as treachery. And you know the penalty for treachery."

Their rooms at the château were self-contained suites, named after people, places, or periods of French history, and decorated appropriately. Sabrina felt specially honored to be Le Roi Soleil, while Pei and Tote, who insisted on sharing Thermidor, were entirely ignorant of the French Revolutionary calendar, but liked the working models of guillotines. Louis Seize was overstylized for C.W., while Graham found Napoleon stark, but militarily compulsive.

As soon as she could, Sabrina slipped along to Louis Seize, and found C.W. in the king-sized bath, decently camouflaged with foam. She perched on the toilet seat, as C.W. groaned and slid even further down into the water. "I know I'm madly attractive," he said, "but couldn't you even wait for me to scrub off?"

"It's not your body I want, C.W.," she grinned. "Not this time, anyway. It's Mike Graham."

"Well why don't you go and sit on his can, then?" C.W. complained, not unreasonably.

Sabrina laughed, and said, "This is serious. Can you stand a drop more water?" He nodded. She turned both taps on, and pulled the toilet flush. Above the noise, she said, "Graham used to be a top man in the CIA. Now he's a defector. He taught me on a weapons course once. He's bound to have recognized me. We could be sunk, finished."

C.W. said, "Oh. Jeeze, I see what you mean." He sat up in the rapidly overflowing tub, and told her he had previously checked the bathroom for bugs, and found none. "So kill the plumbing, will you? Apart from anything else, you've diluted my sarong." Sabrina looked down into the water and said, "So I have. Hey—cute."

She turned off the taps, and asked, "What do we do?"

C.W. made a circular motion with his hand, and she obediently averted her gaze. "OK," he ordered. She looked back. He was in a white terry-cloth robe, patting dry his glowing black skin.

"Has Graham given any sign, anything, that he knows you?" Sabrina shook her head. "But I don't see how he can have failed to recognize me," she insisted.

"OK," C.W. said. "You're probably right. But there's nothing else we can do except play it by ear. If he drops the word to Smith, publicly or privately, we'll know about it soon enough when somebody takes us out to the stables and uses us for target practice. If he doesn't tell Smith, then either you're wrong and he hasn't spotted you, or he's up to some devious little game of his own. In which case we keep cool until we find out what it is. Check?"

"Check. If it's target practice, though, I don't intend to go quietly."

"You're on," C.W. said approvingly. "If I have to go, I'll take Smith with me."

* * *

The castle library was a sumptuous room, paneled in rose-wood, with marvelously embossed cornices and a delicately tinted ceiling. An enormous Indian carpet covered the central well, and there were steps leading to the bookshelves, with trolley-ladders to reach to the highest. Reading desks lit by anglepoise lamps stood in the well, and around them a series of delicate little occasional tables, veneered in rosewood and overlaid with marquetry, sat expectantly before long, cushioned sofas in maroon leather. Drinks and savories were laid out, and the new arrivals waited with Leah and Claude for the Seigneur of Château Clérignault.

As always when Smith was due to appear, Claude prowled the room, checking everything, suspecting everyone, trusting no one. Mike Graham lounged on a chesterfield, sipping white port and munching cheese biscuits topped with Beluga caviar. Sabrina sat as far from him as she could get without arousing suspicion; Pei and Tote inspected the room together, and chuckled over a volume of oriental erotica. C.W. noted with amusement a pamphlet title that read: "TOP SECRET. US ARMY ORDINANCE. BAT GUIDANCE SYSTEM." He picked it up and scanned it. It was genuine.

Smith walked through the open door. He had changed his appearance since Leah last saw him—in the Jacuzzi that morning—and Claude failed to recognize him at first. His hair was now dark brown, his face slightly fuller. He looked taller, younger, more commanding. He was dressed in superbly cut riding clothes, with ludicrously polished boots. He held a riding crop in one hand, methodically tapping the other with the fringed end, and when he spoke it was in the accents of the English upper classes. The white stock at his throat was held in place by a black pearl stickpin.

"Good day to you," he said, "and to those of you whom I have not met before—welcome. I am Mister Smith. Not a strikingly original name, I grant you. Merely the latest, and most adequate for my purposes."

He looked intently from face to face, studying the features, marking their expressions. His gaze lingered on Sabrina, and Leah's lips tightened fractionally. But living with Smith induced chronic fatalism, and she knew that if she had to resign her place in Smith's bed to the ravishing newcomer, she would do so with as good a grace as she could muster, and wait her time.

Only Pei and Tote looked uncomfortable under Smith's prolonged scrutiny. Graham stared nonchalantly back at his host, while C.W. grinned amiably and said, "Hi, there."

"Excellent," Smith beamed—then added to C.W., "Except that when you speak to me, you will always address me as 'Mister Smith.' That rule is invariable. Understood?"

"Sure," C.W. acknowledged. He let fifteen seconds pass, and said, "Uh—Mister Smith."

Smith gave the slightest of bows. "You will be pleased to learn, I am sure, that your identity checks and backgrounds have emerged unsullied from our computers. You are who you claim to be, and you are the people I want for the little scheme I have in mind. However, it is—though important—of little use that I am satisfied with you if, on the other hand, you are dissatisfied with each other, or with me for that matter. Does any of you know, or suspect, something concerning one of the others which you believe could jeopardize my plans? If you do, now is the time to speak."

C.W. tensed his body, and his brain grew ice-cold. Now, he thought; it's now, or never. He checked the position of Claude, whom he calculated was the only armed man in the room. His eyes flickered beyond the library door. The stable yard weapons instructor stood in the hall, arms folded, his back turned to them, a sub-machine gun slung carelessly on his shoulder, finger hovering near the trigger guard.

C.W. let his gaze sweep the room, and saw things he had missed before. The cornice corner moldings concealed television cameras. One of the ceiling bosses was surely a machine gun snout. Or was he getting paranoid? Graham was taking his time, he thought; sadistic bastard.

Mike Graham looked Sabrina full in the eyes. Hers were cast down, but the knowledge that Graham's piercing stare was transfixing her, compelled her to jerk her head up and let her eyes meet his. He gave a half-smile of acknowledgment—and sat back and laced his fingrs together meditatively.

Sabrina felt the breath pumping from her lungs. C.W.

shifted uncomfortably on his aching feet, poised for what had seemed an eternity to take his flying body at Claude's gun, to give them some sort of chance. Mike Graham spoke not a single word. Neither did any other person in the room.

"Again," Smith said, "excellent. We all trust each other. We may even like each other. That helps, I find. No close attachments of course—" His gaze wandered to Pei and Tote. "But friendships, yes."

The tension drained from the room, and Sabrina wondered whether her face had registered the panic which had come so near to erupting when Graham's eyes had pierced her like accusing daggers. Smith spoke again.

"Incidentally, is anyone afraid of heights?" They looked at each other, and shook their heads like marionettes. "Good," Smith went on. "And—C.W., would you have any trouble impersonating a French chef to a French chef? There are black chefs here—I've checked."

C.W. grinned and shook his head afresh. "Un morçeau de gâteau," he replied. Smith laughed, and said to Sabrina, "There's one more pairing which requires specialized skills, that you and Tote possess. It's welding. You'll work together." Sabrina nodded at Tote, who blinked twice.

"I think that takes care of the preliminaries, then," Smith announced, rapping his gloved hand sharply with the riding crop. "More details later, of course. Target, dates, and so on. But for the moment, there's one important piece of information you should have. Indeed, I need it, too. Mr. Graham? Perhaps you would care to tell us what a Lap-Laser is."

Mike sat up and said, "Of course. The Lap-Laser is a tactical self-searching field weapon, laser-armed, auto-recharging—stop me if I'm getting too technical. . . . No? OK. It's lethal to a thousand meters, and it uses a guidance system known as BAT.

"Russia and America have been racing to perfect the gun for years," Mike went on, "but neither had any success until the Americans tried a new element in the guidance system. They discarded the original radar, and substituted lasers to control the gun as well as power it. Now it really works. It's still a little unstable and—shall we say—indiscriminate. But, my God, it works.

"A month ago, the General Electric Corporation of Buffalo, New York State, shipped twelve prototype Lap-Lasers to selected US Army test sites, including one in Europe. The four which were being tested at a secret range near the base at Stuttgart were, unfortunately, stolen. The Army has kept the lid on the theft, and their investigation has been highly confidential, you could say.

"Luckily for us, they were stolen by me. I would imagine they are now here." He looked questioningly at Smith, who nodded. "Great," said Mike. "In that case, whatever our target, however difficult the going is made for us, we have a fantastic edge on anyone trying to stop us. These guns are really something else. They draw enough power to run a small city, and they are so phenomenally destructive that they make the average rocket gun seem like a pea-shooter. With four of them, we could take on an army."

Smith chuckled. "Funny you should say that," he mused. "Because we may have to."

Sabrina and C.W. looked startled. The ponderous Tote cracked his knuckles and beamed.

Despite his promise, Smith decided not to reveal the details of his operation until they had finished what he termed "a short period of training and relocation." Sabrina and C.W. were not too downhearted; there was no possibility, in any case, of getting the information out to Philpott. It troubled them that he almost certainly didn't know where they were, but there was nothing they could do about that, either.

In fact, they were wrong. Philpott knew exactly where they were. Using an Air Force "Blackbird" Mach III spy plane, he had tracked the chopper to the château. Now he was even able to recognize their faces, and photograph them, and Smith and his cohorts. He had seen more of the weaponry at Château Clérignault than C.W. and Sabrina had, and he hadn't liked what he saw. What he didn't know was the final plan and place. And he could think of no way of obtaining that intelligence. He and Sonya Kolchinsky waited—in some comfort—at the Ritz, for Smith to make his move. They dared not risk French or American troops against the laser gun in an assault on the château. They had no option but to play the waiting—and watching—game.

The time passed swiftly enough for Smith's team. The following night, after a tour of the vast estate, Smith assembled them once more in the enclosed stable yard. Claude was relieved to see that the big stallion had slaked his lust and gone to bed.

The evening had been soft and balmy, and all around them was silence. Smith soon stopped that. He gave an airy wave of his hand, the stable doors opened, and the night was filled with deafening noise. The scene was bathed in light from arc-lamps on the roofs and strung to poles overlooking the yard. Smith gestured towards the interior of the stables.

Three monster generator trucks were lined up side by side, under continual cover from ground or aerial surveillance, thick wedges of cable looping from vehicle to vehicle. Further along, banks of turbine generators hummed and flickered with suppressed power. From the last truck, a bunch of cables ran to a wooden platform which had been put up in the yard. The words "RESTAURANT LAROUSSE" were stenciled on the sides of all three trucks.

Smith had assembled practically a hundred other trainees dressed, like his top team, in jumpsuits, to watch the operation. He waved both arms energetically at the truck-drivers, and they cut their engines. "This is a fairly simple but, I feel, impressive demonstration. It is not designed to demonstrate the destructive power of the Lap-Laser guns. If I did that, my beautiful castle would almost certainly be razed to the ground." There was a titter of appreciation, or sympathy, or whatever.

"No. I merely want to show you how the Lap-Laser can combine speed with accuracy and total efficiency. Proceed."

On came the engines again. On the wooden platform, Graham stood at a control panel, all flashing lights and important-looking levers. Three feet away from him, resting on its mounting, black-snouted and menacing, with its mouse-ear detectors ranging edgily, was a Lap-Laser gun. All eyes were fixed on it. Behind Mike, Pei, and C.W. worked at a computer console, monitoring the hit. Tote and Sabrina stood by, engrossed in what they saw.

Graham stood back, patted the Lap-Laser on its stock, and gave a thumbs-up sign to Smith. Smith nodded at

Claude, and Claude pressed a remote-control switch acti-
vating a signal-bulb at the far end of the yard. There, behind a shield of impenetrable lead, four men lifted Russian
Kalashnikov AK 47 rifles, and fired automatic tracers at
orthodox targets in the same area of range that was used
the day before.

Simultaneously, Graham flicked a set of switches on the
panel and a light-beam shot out from the Lap-Lasers. The
tracer rounds screamed across the yard in front of the laser
gun—and disappeared. Working at unbelievable speed, the
Lap-Lasers made minute course and trajectory adjustments,
and each time it blinked—too swiftly that the human eye
could not detect any break in the ray—it selected and
destroyed an individual bullet.

It was a dazzling display of pyrotechnics, and a shattering experience for the spectators. Smith called for quiet
again, and strolled unconcernedly over to the targets. This
time he held a little hand microphone with a trailing lead.

"Not a single round found its mark," he announced in a
matter-of-fact tone. "The Lap-Laser destroyed every one
of them. With four of these to protect us, and to mount
assaults on selected targets, we shall be invulnerable."

Graham manipulated the controls, and the Lap-Laser
subsided. The air was thick with gunsmoke; Mike was
pleased with the outcome of the test. Smith walked across
to the platform and said, "Well done, and thank you."

"Nothing to it," said Graham. Smith asked C.W., "Have
you worked out the safety coding yet?" C.W. replied, "I
think so." He glanced at Sabrina, who had joined Pei and
himself at the computer. Sabrina said, "We think it's tuned
to this at the moment." She indicated a metal tag that C.W.
held in his hand. Graham regarded it curiously.

"Presumably," C.W. said, "it can be set to any metal
alloy for protection, just as it can sniff out and destroy any
predetermined target. But if you don't want it to harm
something, you merely feed into the computer a descrip-
tion and formula of the particular element or alloy to be
avoided. The object—or person—to be protected then
wears a specimen of the embargoed metal, and the Lap-
Laser doesn't function. It will simply miss out that part of
the target altogether."

"Are you sure of this?" Smith inquired.

C.W. nodded, emphatically. "I'd bet my life on it."

"Then why don't you?" drawled Mike Graham.

C.W. smiled, slowly. For a while he made no reply. Then he said, "Do I hear you right, man?" His voice was dangerously low and silky.

"If you didn't," Mike pronounced deliberately, "what I said was: why don't you bet your life on that metal tag?"

C.W. bounced the shiny strip of alloy thoughtfully around his hand. "Why don't I?" he murmured. Then to Graham, "Let's go—fella."

Smith signaled to the truck drivers, and they restarted their engines. Graham manned the control panel, Pei monitored the computer alone. C.W. clipped the metal tag to his breast pocket, and walked the length of the yard to the screen of lead. He waited there, head bowed, until the light blinked fussily above his head.

His step never faltered, but his blood ran ice-cold as he saw Graham trip the Lap-Laser switches. C.W. walked closer and closer to the target area. He felt the hairs of his neck grow individually erect when the barrel of the laser gun turned in his direction. The mouse-ears twitched, picked him up, and locked on to him.

Even above the noise, Sabrina, standing right by the Lap-Laser, heard a dull click as the gun's firing mechanism operated. But there was no fierce glow at the mouth of the tube. No death ray leapt out to reduce the black man to ashes.

"A malfunction?" Smith suggested.

Mike grinned sardonically. He pressed another lever on the panel, and a target silhouette trundled out on the electric pulley until it was bearing down on the area swept by the Lap-Laser. C.W. stopped, looked back, and watched.

The Lap-Laser tracked its new target, discovered no inhibition to firing, and carried out its allotted task. The tube end glowed, the beam flashed once, and the silhouette disintegrated. The trucks were silenced. C.W. turned, and continued his steady march to the platform. He stopped beneath the laser gun, and tossed the safety tag at Graham's feet.

"Don't ever," he hissed, "don't you ever put me on again, boy." He glared at Graham through slit eyes, and Graham looked contemptuously back. C.W.'s fists balled, and his

eyes opened wide, flaring. He stepped aside and commanded, "You! Down here!"

Mike made a move, but Smith's voice cut through their
anger. "Stop! Now!" There could be no argument; they
backed off, glowering. "I have watched your childish exhibition with some interest, not because I particularly care
what happens to either of you, but because it did serve the
purpose of illustrating something else which it is just as
well you should all know.

"You have now had it amply proven that while the Lap-
Laser will destroy indiscriminately what you wish it to
destroy, it will miss any target protected by a safety device
fed into the computer . . . in this case, a metal tag." He
picked the tag up from the platform, and stowed it in his
pocket.

"I have a supply of these tags," Smith continued, "under
lock and key. They will remain there. I have also mounted
a Lap-Laser on the roof of this castle. The way I see it now
is—no unauthorized person can get into the château. And
by the same token, no one can leave. Good night to you."

The following morning, trucks took the main team and a
company of other ranks to a secluded area in the castle
park. They lined up in military formation by a lily pond.
Rising thirty feet above the pond was a tower constructed
mostly of wooden scaffolding poles.

Claude blew a whistle, and the trainees swarmed like
monkeys over the tower; on the bars, through them, inside
and out, some acrobats clinging to the cross-beams by
hands and feet, inching their way along like giant sloths.
Others tightrope-walked on connected pipes, or moved
hand over hand from one side to the other. It looked like
a giant jungle-gym for adults, which was precisely what
it was.

Smith appeared, and motioned to C.W. and Graham. He
held a stopwatch in his hand, and he thumbed it dramatically. At the top of the tower the beams were of metal,
and Sabrina and Tote sat astride a cross-pole, welding
mounts to the iron.

A rope snaked down to drop its end at C.W.'s feet. He
shimmied up it and joined Sabrina on the beam. Below,
Graham fastened the end of the rope to a Lap-Laser. Tote

and C.W. hoisted the gun up the tower, and mounted it on the cross-beam. Then they repeated the operation with a second Lap-Lasèr, which Graham followed until all four trainees were perched on the tower with the two guns. Smith pressed the stopwatch again.

He walked to the foot of the tower and shouted, "Bravo. The best yet. You're improving. It must be the food."

That night in the stable yard, Pei and two other recruits worked under floodlights at the thick bundles of cable. Pei and one of the men wore electricity linemen's heavy-duty gloves. The generators boomed out, and they worked with exaggerated care. Each of the cables bore a lightning bolt label, and the simple warning, "2000 volts."

The gloved trainee, under Pei's watchful gaze, made a long cut in the insulation of the cable. He pried the incision apart with insulated shears, and exposed a section of gleaming copper wire. The second man, who had discarded his gloves, leaned in and opened a huge clamp. It, too, had insulation over its handle and operating nut.

The trainee slid the clamp over the ruptured cable. He was trembling, and his face ran with sweat. Inevitably, his hand slipped and touched the metal of the clamp, which dropped on the exposed cable. A violent blue arc of electricity streaked from the copper wire into the clamp and passed into the body of the unlucky ex-recruit. Pei watched impassively. Then he turned to the other man, and said, "Keep your gloves on. Switch off the current, and get rid of him. And in future, remember: when I say take care, I mean take care."

When the corpse had been removed, and the stench of burning flesh had abated, Pei repeated the maneuver with the clamp—but he made no mistake. He lowered the tool until it barely rested on the copper strands. There was a tiny crackle of current. Nothing more.

So another week of training passed, an endless procession of exercises, weapons practice, written and oral examinations, foot-slogging, fighting; until bone-weary, the team came to what they had been told would be the final day.

They gathered at the lily-pond tower. Graham alone, and again under the tyranny of the stopwatch, approached the scaffolding. Swiftly, he set lumps of plastique and detona-

tors at all four corner supports. He ran back, and peered
over Smith's shoulder at the stopwatch. The hand moved
to zero. The four small explosions flared up, and the tower
collapsed, crashing to the ground in an unruly tangle of
bent piping and broken wooden beams.

Smith was delighted, but didn't explain why.

That night, after dinner in the Great Hall under a glowing crystal chandelier, and eating off silver plates, waited
on like maharajahs, the five newest recruits in Mister
Smith's organization saw him rise to his feet and clap for
silence.

"You have done a fine job during your ten days here,"
he said, "and I am proud of you. You have mastered every
technique necessary for our operation, and you are now at
your peak. It would be pointlessly cruel to keep from you
any longer the details of the project I wish you to undertake, and which I am confident you will discharge with
every success."

So Smith unveiled the master plan. Every detail of it;
coldly, logically, and with great clarity. They listened in
absolute silence as he opened his warped brain to them,
and the appalling lunacies came tumbling out.

"He is mad," C.W. whispered to Sabrina. "God Al-
mighty, he really is."

Mad, perhaps, but not stupid. When Sabrina tentatively
peeped outside her bedroom door just after 1:30 A.M., she
saw two armed guards seated in adjoining chairs halfway
down the stretch of corridor between her room and C.W.'s.
With the secret plan now the common property of all five
new recruits, Smith was clearly taking no chances that any
of them might be foolish enough to consider passing on
their knowledge to the outside.

"Yet somehow," Sabrina murmured furiously, "I've got
to get word to Philpott." She knew he would still be watching the château—that he would have seen the laser guns
and, knowing what he did of their enormous power, would
have ruled out a frontal attack. He could not have spotted
the Restaurant Larousse trucks, which had always been
concealed. He could also know nothing of the target, or the
timing of Smith's scheme. Either she or C.W. must pass

that information to him if there was to be any even remote chance of stopping Smith.

She was sure the guards had not spotted her, but equally aware that she could not get past them undetected. So it would have to be the window. She switched off her bedroom light, leaving the bathroom illuminated so that from the outside it would appear she was taking a late shower. She pulled aside the thick drapes . . . as she expected, searchlights positioned on the crenellated roof coping swept the lawns, gardens, and approach roads. The façade of the château itself was bathed in floodlighting. She could see commandos leashed to trained dogs patroling the grounds.

Sabrina sighed. It would be suicidal to risk flashing a message from her window: one of the patroling commandos would be bound to see it, and she would be unmasked. She opened the window, and peered upwards. Thick, leafy creepers dropped from the eaves to fall down the château walls between the windows.

The searchlights at either end weaved continuously over the manicured lawns and landscaped parkland, but two beams of light from a central point on the roof stayed fixed, trained on the approach road to the château, converging at a distant spot. Sabrina calculated that if she could climb up to the roof unseen, and use one of the fixed lights for signaling, there was a fair chance she would not be spotted from the ground. From the air, though, the message flashed through the intermittently broken beam would be recorded on videotape.

She changed into tight black jeans and a black sweater, and coated her face and hands with mud from the guttering above her dormer window. She glanced to her left: the wall of enveloping creepers was about six feet away. She eased her body over the windowsill, stood upright, pressing her face to the rough, hard stone of the wall, and crab-walked the ledge until she reached the shelter of the ivy and Virginia creeper.

She burrowed into the dusty, spiderwebbed area behind the impenetrable waterfall of green and red leaves, and used the cover to climb up to the battlemented roof coping. She scaled the wall linking the two turrets, and lay panting in the fork between the battlements and the sloping roof.

To either side of her, the big end-mounted searchlights kept up their sweeping pattern. The two smaller, fixed lights were on the apex of the roof between nests of chimneys, a little to her right.

Sabrina marveled at the fantastic towers and turrets strewn across the roof and battlements, darker than the house below them but still sufficiently lit to throw grotesque shadows on the tiles. She squirmed along to a patch of deeper shadow and, inch by inch, started the long crawl up the roof.

Small twin campaniles stood at either end of the roof, and from the open spaces above the bell mountings, eight bright and beady eyes looked out between the slim stone pillars and monitored her progress. . . .

Sabrina froze as she felt the beating of wings on the air, terrifyingly close to her face. The pair of shaheen peregrine falcons, one an eyas, trained from the nest, the other haggard, caught wild, had taken to the air fractionally before the matched pair of Greenland gerfalcons from the opposite belltower. They were both eyasses, and, like the peregrines, females. The female hunting hawk is a third larger than the tiercel, or male, and the gerfalcon is the biggest of the game-taking hawks.

The peregrines soared high above the château, and the eyas made the first dive, dropping almost perpendicularly, then flattening out in a swooping dive that took her unsheathed claws to within eighteen inches of Sabrina's disbelieving eyes. The haggard peregrine followed her, legs and claws extended, beak open in an eldritch screech, her whole body aimed like a deadly live projectile. Sabrina choked back a scream as the hawk's mottled belly flashed before her face, and one of the tufted wingtips brushed her hair.

She jerked up her head and saw, with relief, the two hunting birds climbing away in a high arc above her. Then a second throaty squawk assailed her from the right, and the first of the monstrous, white-plumed gerfalcons bore down on her from the night sky. She rolled over, and the gerfalcon's claws scraped the tiles where her face had been.

Terror overwhelmed her mind, and she slipped and bumped her way down the eight feet of roof she had climbed to lay hunched in the angle of the battlements.

Even so, she was not quick enough for the second ger-falcon, which altered course at the last moment and, as Sabrina upended herself in her tumbling flight, took a quarter-inch strip of flesh away from her left ankle.

She could see all four hawks now, circling overhead to dive for what she suspected would be a concerted attack. Worse, shouts from below told her that Smith's airborne guard dogs had been spotted by a patrol.

Sabrina guessed she had one chance left: if the attention of the armed commandos was fixed on the hawks, she might be able to squeeze unobserved between the fortified battlements and drop to the creepers.

A third grating screech was all the warning she needed. As the haggard peregrine started its dive, Sabrina slithered over the eaves and dropped head first into the nest of creepers.

Her clutching hands found thick bundles of liana, and she broke her fall, twisted around, and prayed that the creepers would support her weight. Dust flew, wall-roots tore apart and the spiders danced unaccustomed nocturnal capers—but the creepers held. Sabrina got her breath back, and hauled herself up to the ledge.

She looked out between the leaves, and saw with a sinking heart that she was still far away from her own window, which she had left unobtrusively ajar. Then the window nearest her squeaked open, and C.W. hissed, "Swing over here, you silly cow!"

Sabrina grasped a bunch of ivy and wooded liana and launched herself into space. She landed in C.W.'s arms feet first, and he grabbed her body and hauled her into his darkened bathroom. He slammed the window shut, and said to her brusquely, "Strip."

Meekly, Sabrina did as she was told. . . .

Ten minutes later, bathed and coiffured, Sabrina sat demurely on a chaise longue in the Louis Seize suite. C.W. answered the peremptory knock at the door.

Smith stood there, flanked by armed guards. His eyes took in the nonchalant black, clearly naked under the terry-cloth robe; they shifted to Sabrina who, equally clearly, was wearing only a bath towel.

"My guards tell me," Smith began, "that the hawks have

been active. They believe someone came into a room on
this floor, possibly from the roof. Could it have been either
of you?" He let the question hang dangerously in the air.

"It could have been," C.W. shrugged, then adding, seemingly as an afterthought. "Sir."

"In fact, it was," Sabrina put in. Smith raised his eyebrows in her direction.

She went on calmly, "Since you chose, for reasons of
your own, Mister Smith, to make us prisoners, I took it as
a challenge, a point of honor almost, to sneak along the
ledge outside my room and see my friend C.W."

"For what purpose, may I ask?" Smith inquired.

Sabrina simpered. "When I'm dressed like this?" she said,
letting the towel slip further down her shoulders. "Really,
Mister Smith, you either have very little imagination or
you lead an abnormally sheltered life here."

Smith looked steadily at her, weighing the evidence.
"My guards didn't see you," he pointed out.

"The wall was completely lit up," Sabrina countered,
"bathed, you could say, in white light."

"So?"

"So I was naked. Camouflage—n'est-ce-pas?"

Smith's stony face relaxed into a grin. "Now that's the
kind of audacity I admire. Well, assuming you have finished what you came here to do, Sabrina—" she nodded,
and C.W. winked. "Good," Smith went on, "in that case,
let me escort you back to your own room by a route con-
siderably less arduous and dangerous than the one you
selected for the outward trip."

She rose to her feet, and let the towel drop to the floor.
"Thanks C.W.—for everything," she said.

Smith's eyes combed her naked body. "I trust my little
falcons didn't treat you too badly, Sabrina," he said.

She showed him her blood-spotted ankle. "Hardly anything," she replied.

Smith tutted solicitously. "Dear, dear," he murmured,
"I hope they don't get a taste for human flesh."

CHAPTER
SEVEN

Sonya Kochinsky rose early and walked from the most celebrated and luxurious hotel in Paris into the most harmonious square in that city of beautiful proportions, Place Vendôme. She strolled through the markets, and then embarked on a determined window-shopping spree, from the Rue du Faubourg St-Honoré through Rue Castiglione, crossing to Boulevard Haussmann, and on through Boulevard Batignolles and Boulevard Courcelles to the Arc de Triomphe.

She took the bus down Avenue Kleber to the Palais de Chaillot, and trekked back across the river, past the Eiffel Tower, to the Boulevard Garibaldi. She checked her watch: it was still only eight-fifteen.

Sonya found the side street at the rear of the École Militaire, and saw the unsalubrious little workmen's café. It was three-quarters full. The atmosphere was compounded about equally of coffee, croissants, Disque Bleue, and Caporal. Two sweatshirted laborers sat at the corner table, and it was there that she headed.

Sonya approached the table uncertainly. One workman was eyeing his cognac with practiced relish; the other had his face plunged into a newspaper. She peered over the top of the paper. This man also had a cognac in front of him. He wore a greasy cap, and printed on his T-shirt was the legend, "APRÉS MOI LE DÉLUGE." "Sit down, then," Philpott said. She lowered herself into the spare seat, and was made embarrassingly aware that she was dressed a shade formally for "La Chatte qui siffle" on a busy September midweek morning.

"Cats," she said tartly to Philpott, "do not whistle." Without looking up from his newspaper, Philpott drawled, "In here, baby, they do as they're told." Their neighbor got up to leave, and wished them "bon appétit" with a knowing leer. Sonya tossed her well-groomed head and ordered coffee and croissants. They were, as she suspected, delicious.

Philpott laid down the paper. "To business," he said. "I didn't wake you last night, but I had a call at about 2 A.M. They're on the move. Or, at least, the chopper and half a dozen trucks left in the small hours. And that is a Lap-Laser on the roof of the château, or rather, was. It's gone now. The game, as Holmes probably never said, is afoot."

"And still nothing from Sabrina or C.W.," Sonya said, bitterly.

"You've checked?" Philpott asked. She nodded. "On the way here, and back at the Ritz. The stations, the Élysée —everywhere. Not a single word. We don't even know if they're alive."

"If Graham has denounced Sabrina, then she'll certainly be dead," Philpott muttered, grimly, "and I can't see C.W. letting that happen, without getting involved. So . . . we must be prepared for the worst."

Sonya drained her first cup of coffee, and set the cup down with a nervous clatter. "And we still don't know his target, where he's going to strike, or when. Or anything, really." She looked beseechingly into Philpott's eyes. "Have we lost, Malcolm—lost out to Smith? And sacrificed C.W. and Sabrina into the bargain? Has it all been for nothing?"

Philpott placed his hand over hers. He shook his head. "No," he whispered. "We haven't lost yet. We're some way down, but we're far from out." He rose to his feet and put two ten-franc bills on the table. "Come on," he said, "I'm fed up with slumming. Let's go back to the hotel. At least we'll be in touch there."

Sonya got up. "I never did find out why you picked this place for a meeting at this ungodly hour," she remarked.

"I'll tell you back at the hotel," he promised.

They turned into Boulevard Garibaldi, and right again past the École Militaire into the Champ de Mars. Philpott stopped to light a pleasant-smelling cheroot, and glanced upwards.

The trite and infuriatingly ugly bulk of the Eiffel Tower completely filled his vision.

Tote and Pei left the table they had been occupying by the door of "La Chatte qui siffle," and took the same path Philpott and Sonya had taken a few minutes before. They, too, looked up at the Eiffel Tower, and Pei grinned happily at Tote. They traversed the Champ de Mars, and crossed the busy intersection to reach the foot of the tower.

It is difficult to imagine any construction as crass as the Eiffel Tower being erected to mark the dawn of the age of technology, but that indeed was the driving force behind the eccentric French engineer, Gustave Alexandre Eiffel, in the late 1880s. Eiffel greatly admired the American inventors Thomas Alva Edison and Alexander Graham Bell, and worked for two years to design possibly the ugliest, but most charming, commemorative monument in history.

Eiffel used five thousand yard-square sheets of paper for his *full-scale* plan of the tower, but at least by the time he had finished there could be only one answer to the ludicrous question: what's made of two and a half million rivets and twelve thousand pieces of metal, weighs fifteen million pounds, stands nearly a thousand feet tall, and looks like a giraffe?

The tower was inaugurated on June 10, 1889, by Prince Bertie of England, later King Edward VII, who, it was doubtless said at the time, should have known better. Later, though, when successful wireless experiments were carried out between the tower and the Panthéon, Eiffel's éléphant blanc was used as a radio broadcasting tower.

Gustave Eiffel could not have foreseen it, but would doubtless have been pleased that the tower now doubles as a television transmitter. At the moment it is 984 feet, 6 inches high, but with the Eiffel Tower, you never can tell. The German occupying forces in Paris during World War II considered requisitioning the tower and turning it, presumably, into tanks, but in the end the plan proved to be either sacrilegious or too much trouble.

Apart from the fact that the face of Paris would today be unthinkable without the tower, its undeniably most use-

ful function is one that probably never occurred to Eiffel:
the peak provides one of the most astonishing views on
earth.

From the quaint little encircling balcony at the top, the
daytime shadow falls across the Champ de Mars (where
Napoleon used to review his troops) and the École Militaire. The military school was the creation of an unlikely
trio: the financier, Paris-Duverney; Madame Pompadour;
and the playwright, Beaumarchais. Below the tower is the
River Seine, behind it the superb Palais de Chaillot, with
its gardens and ornamental fountains. The feet of the tower
plunge into the woodland, spanned by the access road.
There are fountains in the foreground, too, and everywhere broad, sweeping avenues of pavement and grass;
theaters, museums, palaces . . . Paris.

Pei and Tote skirted the balloon seller, and passed
through the light morning crowd to the entrance of the
tower. The balloon-man was doing a fair trade—some
tribute, no doubt, to the fact that Michael Graham had
filled balloons before, and was used to handling gas. He
put a shot of hydrogen into a long, knobbly, purple job,
and handed it to an ecstatic little Dutch girl.

"Whirrrrr-click!" went the automatic shutter of an expensive camera around the neck of a tourist. Smith was
dressed in a well-cut lightweight suit with matching tie
and pocket handkerchief, and sensible brogues; to avoid
confusing his troops, he had kept the same face.

Smith took another picture, sighting through the central
arch of the tower towards the Palais de Chaillot. He strolled
unconcernedly to the waiting elevator. He boarded it, and
as it soared upwards, he stood gazing vacantly into space,
with an imbecilic expression on his face, as tourists often
do. On the far side of the elevator, Sabrina and Claude
chatted animatedly about nothing in particular.

The elevator reached the first, and widest, landing, and
Smith got out. Another, less expensive, camera clicked.
Leah Fischer, elbows balancing on the rail, squinted
through the eyepiece and took a second meaningless snap.
She ignored Smith when he brushed against her as he
passed. Pei and another member of the commando team,
dressed in business suits, rounded the gallery; Pei was deep

into a clipboard of technical papers; his companion pointed occasionally, and made helpful comments.

The elevator reached the first landing again on its way down. A burly, powerful workman got out; he was in overalls, with oil-stained hands. He was on his morning coffee break—rather ahead of time, considering—and he walked to the rail next to Leah.

"It's OK," Tote grunted. "We're ready." And he nodded in the direction of the private, commercial access road to the Eiffel Tower.

The three "RESTAURANT LAROUSSE" generator trucks trundled to the foot of the tower, and moved into position near a service elevator. A white-coated chef climbed stiffly from the cab of the leading vehicle, stretched prodigiously, and winked at the balloon seller. "Sassy idiot," Graham muttered, but C.W. was too far away to hear.

One of the tower guards stepped from his office and spoke to the tall-hatted black chef. A pantechnicon and a smaller van had joined the generator trucks. A team of workmen busily, and very swiftly, unloaded crates, steam-boxes, brightly colored beer tanks, portable stoves, and microwave ovens—a bewildering mass of equipment.

The guard surveyed the mountain range of boxes. "Open the crates, please," he directed the chef, who had presented a perfect set of documents explaining everything.

"Open the crates!" C.W. expostulated. "The steam-boxes, the sealed containers? You want me to ruin my soufflés? You want dust in my sauces? You want my bombe surprise to melt? That is either a joke in extremely bad taste, Monsieur, or you are irretrievably unhinged."

Ignoring him, the guard pried off the lid of a steam-box. C.W. closed his eyes, and muttered a prayer to the patron saint of haute cuisine. Neat rows of unbaked bread, flûte alternating with baguette, stared up at the custodian.

"Don't even breathe," C.W. snarled, gently closing the case. "They must rest—like innocent children. Their labors are barely begun—while yours, Monsieur, may be coming to an untimely but completely justified end!"

Graham regarded the scene with amusement, tinged with reluctant admiration. C.W. again caught his eye. Mike looked away, clutched the balloon strings in his hand more tightly, then leapt up in frustration as a yellow balloon escaped and floated into the air. He shook his free fist at it, and cursed volubly, but in fairly restrained language. C.W. wasn't the only one who could put on a convincing act, he thought smugly.

The guard surveyed the hopelessness of his task. He couldn't possibly open every one of the bound crates, and the chef was becoming too overbearing for words, stamping around him in a circle and heaping culinary curses on his undeserving head.

"Eh bien—allez!" he said, resignedly. C.W. triumphantly gathered his team and trophies around him, and they commenced loading the service elevator.

At the rail of the lower gallery, Smith had swapped his camera for a pair of binoculars, and panned over the view below. He locked on to the yellow balloon as it rose skywards against the glorious panorama of Paris. He took the binoculars from his eyes, and a half-smile played on his lips.

Then he raised the glasses once more, his gaze wandering further out, to the river. He ranged over the bateaux mouches, the sightseeing boats of the Seine that ply up and down the river between April and October, on hour-long trips. He picked up, too, a flotilla of Tour Eiffel vedettes, the smaller, eighty-two seater, glass-topped motor boats, which started from the Pont d'Iéna, near the tower, or the Quai Montebello. The bateaux mouches leave from the Right Bank, at the Pont de l'Alma.

Smith fixed the precise location of the particular bateau mouche for which he had been searching, and once more grinned his satisfaction.

The service elevator drew up at the gallery. C.W. stepped importantly out, chef's hat aquiver, and stood with arms folded, casing the scene. He directed that his mass of equipment, now borne on stout-wheeled trolleys, should be taken into the restaurant kitchen facing him. A brace of commandos jumped forward to hold open the swinging doors. Inside the restaurant itself, C.W. could see a French television crew, from RTF, setting up cameras and lights to cover a news event.

Smith, still at the rail, but now standing next to Leah as the crowds on the tower began to thicken, peered through the binoculars at the press of people swarming around the tower entrance. Claude, who had descended some time before, was waiting to come back up. Smith spotted other commandos in the crowd, dressed as tourists, workmen, waitresses (for Sabrina Carver was far from being the only woman on the team) and other employees of the tower.

Mister Smith murmured to Leah, "Let me know when everyone's up here." Perhaps three minutes later, she touched his arm tentatively, and whispered, "All present and correct, sir."

The urgent wail of a police-car siren penetrated the hubbub. Smith swung around at the rail, and brought the glasses to his eyes. A limousine, one of the largest and grandest at the disposal of the French government, turned into the tower access road. It was preceded by two armed motorcycle outriders, flanked by two more and trailed by a further pair. The Doppler effect scaled the siren down an octave, and the noise stopped altogether as the car drew to a halt.

A man stepped out, and shut the car door behind him. Even from the gallery perch, Smith could see the bulge of the gun in the visitor's left armpit. The Secret Service agent looked carefully around him, then up at the tower, then down again, his eyes hunting the scattering of people, his hands and shoulders twitching.

From the other side of the car, a second agent got out, slammed the door, and repeated the scrutiny his colleague had already made. They glanced at each other and, on a nod from the first agent, the second opened the car door on his side, and politely ushered out a tall, handsome woman in her late sixties or early seventies.

The four men in the official welcoming committee detached themselves from the tower entrance, and hurried forward. In the van was a small, round, flustered type, in morning coat and striped trousers, bare-headed. He beamed distractedly (he always beamed distractedly) at the dignified lady, and said, "My dear Mrs. Wheeler. What an honor for us! What a great pleasure and privilege! What a truly glorious day this is for the Eiffel Tower, for the Children's Relief Fund, for France, for—"

"Monsieur Verner, how very nice to see you again," Adela Wheeler cut in. "On the contrary, it was kind of you to invite me, and I'm glad to be here."

Bertrand Verner stammered his profuse thanks, and introduced her to the other dignitaries of the tower and of the International Children's Relief Fund. She met them graciously, her strong mellifluous voice speaking in scarcely accented French or, when prompted, in western seaboard American, but so unassumingly upper-crust that it could have been Bostonian or southern standard English.

French security men stood in a discreet ring behind the official party, and they divided to let through Mrs. Wheeler and her guards, who were guided into the elevator to make the trip alone to the first floor. True to form, the Secret Service calculated that the fewer people close to their charge at any one time, the better.

In the kitchen of the tower restaurant, where the lunch-time fund-raising banquet was to be held, all was controlled chaos under the regular chef, Albert. The last thing Albert wanted was for the doors to burst open, and a rival chef enter, pursued by seemingly dozens of assistant chefs and waiters bearing impossible cargoes of equipment. But Albert had been prepared for the intrusion of the Restaurant Larousse, specialists in outside catering, though he still regarded C.W.'s presence with resentment and hostility.

Albert watched in silence as C.W. commandeered his kitchen, and muttered at one point, "Tiens! Warmed-up food. Pffft!"

C.W. spun around on him. "Warmed up? WARMED UP? Here, my peasant friend," he indicated a stack of steaming boxes, "here are *cooking*, not warming, *cooking*, fifty and more light and incomparable *Soufflés aux Crevettes demoules* in modulated microwaves. *Here*, idiot, are braising truffles in *Sauce Brune aux Fines Herbes*. Do you call that warming up? Hein?"

Albert shrugged, and made as if to open a case. C.W. administered a hefty slap to his wrist and snapped, "Ne touchez pas," like to a naughty child.

Inside the restaurant, the also-rans were waiting to welcome their undisputed guest of honor. Smith whispered to Claude, who sidled out to the corridor and sent the service elevator back down. Beneath the fork of the tower, an ice-cream vendor opened his icebox and produced two machine-pistols. He handed one to Mike Graham, who barged into the tower guard's office.

The guard saw Mike's gun, and made for his own. Graham caught him by the front of his uniform, dragged him over the guardroom counter, and brutally pistol-whipped him. Then he herded the guard and the elevator operator into the service elevator and took it up.

The main elevator now stopped at the restaurant level, the operator opened the gate, and Mrs. Wheeler's two Secret Service agents led her into the corridor. Claude's ambush was sudden and appallingly savage.

He felled the first agent with a vicious groin kick. The second man was going for his weapon, but his arm was seized by another commando, and Claude, in a movement that was purely balletic, whirled and lashed out another kick from the rear. It caught the agent in the gut, and a swing with a lead-tipped truncheon from a commando ended his interest in the affair.

Back in the kitchen, C.W. rounded once more on Albert, and snorted, "Now, my fine friend, I will show you—my pièce de résistance." He tapped the lid of a formidably large catering case. Albert's eyes followed the movement.

The lid of the case flew up, and C.W. calmly handed out to his team a succession of wicked-looking MA-28 Meisner machine-pistols and Thompson machine guns. C.W. waved at Albert with the snout of a gun. "Up," he commanded. The chef and his entire staff shot their arms into the air, and stood rigid as statues. C.W. chuckled. "I bet this is the craziest entrée *you've* ever seen, Albert, old son," he said in English. Albert goggled.

C.W.'s men were already pushing napkin-draped trolleys into the restaurant, and peeling off the cloths to reveal an assortment of dangerous hardware, when Smith walked up to Mrs. Wheeler and announced, in a pleasant and neutral voice, "Good afternoon, Mrs. Wheeler. I am Mister Smith. I regret to tell you that you are my prisoner. If you will accompany this young lady"—he indicated Leah—"without too much trouble, I guarantee that you will come to no harm whatsoever."

Adela Wheeler gazed steadily at him. "I presume," she said, "that you know who I am."

Smith nodded acquiescence. "If I did not," he pointed out, "I would hardly have gone to all the trouble of kidnapping you."

Adela Wheeler still regarded him stonily. "You cannot, of course, hope to get away with this foolish and disastrous crime. You will be made to pay for it; of that you can be certain." Smith looked at her admiringly; she was dignity personified, exquisitely gowned, her grey hair piled in bouffant waves, her face imperious and haughty, unafraid, scornful.

"Please," Smith gestured towards Leah. "You will be comfortable, and unmolested, in the VIP room."

"I know the room well," Mrs. Wheeler rejoined, "whereas I honestly doubt whether you have ever been inside it—or would be welcomed there if you did." She turned on her heel, brushed Leah aside, and walked firmly out of the restaurant.

The dining-room commandos spread out and herded the guests into a corner at gunpoint. Graham and his ice-cream vendor arrived, with members of the tower staff under guard. On the second landing, far above their heads, other commandos poured out of the elevators and trained their guns on the tourists. A guard rushed to an alarm button, but was cut down by a burst of fire from a Kalashnikov.

Pei shouted through a megaphone. "No one is to move. Stand absolutely still. Do not try to be heroes. You will die if you do."

The elevator continued its deadly journey. The top observation platform, at the very summit of the tower below the television mast, was only lightly peopled. The assault team took it with ease, disarming and trussing up the defeated guards.

In the first-level restaurant, C.W. unlocked a catering crate marked "Microwave Oven P769/521 COOKFAST." He called Mike Graham over, and together they tenderly lifted out a darkly gleaming Lap-Laser. Up aloft by the rail of the second gallery, three men just as carefully hoisted Sabrina Carver over the side of the tower. She wore a welding mask, and someone handed to her an acetylene torch and a stout iron bracket. Sabrina got to work . . . and she was a fast worker.

Mrs. Wheeler sat in a comfortable chair in the VIP room, hands clasped to stop them trembling. She had resolutely refused to speak to Leah who had locked the door and left. She had no idea what Mister Smith required of her—apart from the obvious ransom for her release. She suspected, though, that he had chosen the location badly. If she was trapped on the Eiffel Tower, then so was he. She had a premonition—which, surprisingly, was not too distasteful—that she would not survive the day.

Tourists arrived in droves from above, and huddled together on the gallery, and in the open spaces and restaurant, as Smith took a megaphone and addressed them. "All visitors and tower personnel, listen to me. You will be released safe and unharmed if you do not panic, and if you do precisely as you are instructed. You will shortly enter the elevators in small groups, as directed by my staff. Once on the ground, please leave the area of the tower immediately. If you do not, you will place yourself in very grave danger indeed. Now—get to the elevators, and wait your turn as my men tell you."

Sabrina, perched precariously on the scaffolding of the tower midway between the first and second levels, put the finishing touches to her bracket welding. From the landing below, Mike peered out and saw her. He signaled to C.W., who ran to join him. "There she goes," Mike said, and he and the black man took the Lap-Laser over the rail and knotted the rope around it. A commando team from above began to haul it on its long trip up the side of the tower.

Police and bystanders stood in anxious groups watching with mounting curiosity as the slim black gun rose into the air, hugging the girders. Sabrina looked down on the swaying Lap-Laser with equal concern. She knew what the crowd didn't know: that any hard knock from the metal struts to the delicate firing mechanism—particularly to the circular, side-mounted radar detectors—could put the wonder-weapon out of commission. Sabrina muttered a

silent prayer that if it was going to happen, it should happen quickly—before the need arose for her to fumble the
bolting of the laser gun to its bracket.

For that was the plan she had in mind: a last, desperate
bid to immobilize at least one of Smith's toys and even up
the odds for Philpott.

But the gun reached Sabrina safely, and as the commandos detached it from its sling, she steeled herself
to drop it back down the tower. Then Smith's voice floated
down to her. "No slips now, Sabrina. I shall hold you
personally responsible if anything happens to that gun."

In the maintenance areas, Pei and his band of electronic
specialists were tapping into the main power cables supply-
ing the tower, as Pei had shown them in the practice ses-
sions at the Château Clérignault. This time, there were no
accidents, and within minutes, stewardship of the electricity
supply to the entire tower and its environs had passed into
Pei's capable hands.

The first tourists were leaving the tower. They streamed
away, ignoring the incoming policemen brought there by
the sudden lack of communication with the tower, by
isolated bursts of gunfire, and by the fact that the security
men augmenting Mrs. Wheeler's guards had failed to report.
Women in the crowd sobbed as they tried to cope with
hysterical children. Men looked back grimly, and talked
excitedly among themselves of their good fortune in getting
away. The policemen pushed impatiently at the elevator
buttons, but there was no response. Pei had seen to that.
He was now the Eiffel Tower's sole elevator operator.

The steel-helmeted riot police arrived, all shields, blast-
guns and machismo. They listened to the tragic tales of the
common flics, then grouped in a spearhead at the entrance
to the tower, and rushed the stairs. Their shields, however,
proved not to be impervious to high-velocity, armor-
piercing bullets, and they retreated in disorder, leaving
dead and wounded littering the steps.

Smith heard the shooting as he descended to his command position near the first-landing elevators. "Keep it to
the minimum," he yelled through the megaphone to the
group manning the stairs. "Tell that to the riot cops,"
called out a commando.

Smith turned inquiringly to one of his principal lieutenants, who supplied the commando's name. "He did not
address me correctly," Smith said, in a voice so urbane that
it chilled his subordinate, "and he was impertinent. When
the operation is concluded, shoot him. Through the spine.
Make sure he lives."

The tower was clearing fast now. The only people Smith
kept there under lock and key were the more daring among
the guards—those who still lived, that is—and the security
men of both nationalities, who were beaten senseless as a
precaution.

On the rusty-red iron scaffolding members, Sabrina
Carver and C.W. Whitlock clamped a third Lap-Laser gun
into place. Another team, led by Pei, handled the fourth
and last dreaded super-weapon on the opposite flank. Smith
assembled his entire task force on "level one," and handed
over temporarily to Leah. She took a large bundle of
metal tags from a box.

"You all know what these are," Leah said. "They're laser
safety tags. Wear them at all times, please. It's probably
unnecessary to caution you about this, since you all know
what will happen to you if you don't wear them. We'll be
arming the Lap-Lasers in a very few moments. In case you
have any remaining doubts about their powers, let me
assure you that they will automatically destroy anything
that moves on this tower, or near it, which doesn't have
one of these metal protective code tags. I'll hand out the
tags now. After that, it's up to you."

"Thank you, Leah," said Smith, taking the tag she
offered him, and pinning it ostentatiously to his breast on
the lapel of his suit. "I'll see you in the restaurant when
we've set up.'

"I wouldn't miss it for the world, Mister Smith," she
replied.

The last load of tourists left the tower, and scampered
away to join the crowd, now held in check by a police
cordon at a respectful distance. On his way back to the
restaurant, Smith peered over the side cautiously. He had
instructed his commandos to keep well out of sniping
range; once the laser-guns were operative, they would, of
course, have no need to observe such caution.

The scene was bizarre, looking upwards or downwards.

Going up, the sole occupants of the Eiffel Tower above
the first level were pigeons, gulls, and smaller birds. They
wheeled in and out of the stanchions and cross-members,
and buzzed the top observation platform like Macbeth's
temple-haunting martlets.

Below, there was a cordon sanitaire around the tower.
Nothing inside it moved. Traffic had been halted, the access
roads and main junction were sealed off, the walkways
from the Champ de Mars and the Palais de Chaillot
cleared, even of animals. The fountains were stilled, and
every eye in the vast and growing crowd turned upwards
in tribute, Smith's mad brain told him, to his remarkable
genius.

He withdrew, and walked towards the restaurant. As he
reached the door, Pei stepped forward and delivered the
crucial message. "The Lap-Lasers are fully armed and
functioning, Mister Smith." Smith replied, "Excellent, Pei,
excellent."

The central command post had been set up in the
restaurant, and apart from the busy commando leaders,
probably the most valued people there were the French
television crew, who were destined to play in the drama
a role of which none of them had dreamed when they left
that morning on a routine assignment.

Under Pei's direction, and to Mike Graham's secret
amusement, cables had been dragged in bunches into the
cleared dining area, and the little bandstand was now the
setting for a bank of TV monitors, covering every aspect
around the tower. A group of three color monitors stood
to one side, showing, for the moment, RTF test cards.
Smith looked appraisingly at the scene, occasionally glanc-
ing at his stopwatch.

Finally, he summoned the French TV cameraman who,
like most continental network operators, used a small,
portable ENG (Electronic News Gathering) camera, rather
than the unwieldly Arrieflexes and other film cameras
of old.

"You will operate the ENG camera at my direction, and
inject straight into the network, as you have been instructed?" Smith asked.

"Oui, Monsieur," the man replied.

"If you do not," Smith warned, "or if in any way you

attempt to cross me ... I have no need, I am sure, to tell you what will happen to you."

The cameraman assured him hastily that he would do as he was told. "No tricks, Monsieur," he added, "I have a wife and kids, and RTF does not pay me enough to die for them."

"Good," Smith returned. "Then make the preparations."

"What exactly is it you wish me to do, Monsieur?" queried the technician.

"That's simple," Smith said. "I want to make a broadcast to the world. I want to tell them that I have stolen the Eiffel Tower, and that I am holding as my prisoner the mother of the President of the United States of America."

CHAPTER EIGHT

Sonya ordered lunch to be sent up to Suite 701, and the Ritz's room service obliged with omelettes, side salads, light desserts, and a bottle of Chablis. Neither she nor Philpott were in the mood to sample the celebrated déjeuner mondain or the delights of the Espadon Grill.

They had not been idle during the morning. Philpott maintained a steady contact with the message drop-points in Paris, with INTERPOL and the Sureté, with the Elysée Palace, and with the CIA and the duty monitor at UNACO. So far, they had drawn blanks.

As he forked the first slice of omelette into his mouth, the telephone rang again. "Always happens," he grunted, "usually when I'm in the shower."

Philpott picked up the receiver, announced himself, and listened for perhaps three minutes in total silence.

Then he said, "God in Heaven, François, I expected it to be bad, but nothing like this. Hang on a sec." He gestured towards the corner of the lavishly decorated room, where vast windows offered breathtaking views of Paris. "Sonya, switch on the television set," he said, urgently. Then back to the telephone. "Go on please, François."

Philpott listened again, fired a couple of quick questions, made notes on a scribbling pad next to the telephone, and finally said, "Me? I'll get hold of the Ambassador right away. I know more about Smith than probably anyone else alive. I shall be pleased to help. Indeed, I insist on offering my services. Thank you. Au Revoir."

He replaced the telephone as the color TV screen flickered into life. "For God's sake, Malcolm, tell me what's happened," Sonya cried in exasperation. "The worst," Philpott answered. "The very worst. Smith, would you believe, has hijacked the Eiffel Tower—or so the police say . . . that was François LeMaître, from the Sureté."

"Hijacked the Eiffel Tower?" Sonya echoed, incredulously.

"Taken it with an armed force. But that's not all. By Christ, that's in no way everything."

"What do you mean?"

"He's got a hostage, Sonya, and I have no doubt whatsoever that in his insanity, he will not hesitate to sacrifice the hostage if things go against him."

"Who is it, Malcolm?"

"Someone whose life we cannot afford to hazard," Philpott said, dully. "It's Warren's mother, Sonya. Adela Wheeler, mother of Warren G. Wheeler, President of the United States of America."

The color drained from her face. "Wh-what—what—"

"What's she doing here?" Philpott supplied. "She's over on invitation from the International Children's Relief Fund —you know, it's her pet charity. There's a fund-raising lunch, at the Eiffel Tower—today."

"God"—he smashed his fist into his palm—"how could I have overlooked that? How could I have been so stupid as not to check that, when Lorenz van Beck as good as told me it was the Eiffel Tower?"

"Van Beck did?" Sonya queried.

Philpott nodded, and ran his fingers through his hair. He wrenched open his top collar button and pulled down his tie. "Yeah," he murmured, disconsolately. "As van Beck said: what else has two and a half million rivets? I believed him, of course . . . that's why we went to that little café this morning—just on the off-chance that I might see something, or someone, which would give us a lead. But some hopes," he snorted in self-disgust. "Even if I'd tripped over Smith himself, I would probably have had a nice chat and bought him a beer."

Sonya rose and went to him. "Quitting?" she asked. "Self-pity's not your line, Philpott. Fight back, or we're lost. Please?" She straightened his tie, and smoothed back his hair. Then she noticed, past his shoulder as he held her and kissed her cheek, the TV set purring away in the corner.

Over the domestic tribulations of a particularly involved French soap opera a message repeatedly flashed: "EMERGENCY INTERRUPT." Sonya broke free with a start. "Look, Malcolm," she said, "something's coming on TV about it, I think."

Philpott turned, and studied the set. Then he crossed the room and sat on a chaise longue within comfortable distance. "It's Smith," he explained to Sonya. "Apparently he's got himself a link straight into RTF from the tower. His communications boys have arranged it so that the Post Office can't stop him, even if they wanted to. And at the moment, the French Government doesn't want to stop him. Let's hear what he's got to say."

Sonya joined him. The emergency signal became a permanent fixture as the trivial soap opera faded. After a minute the stark message blinked out, and the screen cleared. The next image on French and continental Western European television was the face of Mister Smith.

"I am sorry," Smith began, "to interrupt your normal television fare, but, as compensation, I bring you a real-life drama which I hope you will find even more absorbing." He spoke in faultless French, and repeated the sentence in English.

He continued, "My name is Mister Smith, and I have just stolen the Eiffel Tower. No, I'm not joking. See for yourselves."

The screen cut to another camera, which roamed the tower, concentrating on the first level, seeking out the armed guards, then wandering below, to the cordon of frustrated police, and the seething crowd. It avoided the laser-guns, and for a moment Philpott's heart leapt: perhaps something had gone wrong. Perhaps C.W. and Sabrina had managed to immobilize the Lap-Lasers, to give the authorities at least a fighting chance. . . . But then he reflected, "No, the bastard's just playing with us."

"You see now, do you?" Smith said triumphantly. "I am speaking the truth. And that is not all. I have a prisoner here on the tower—a hostage, if you like, although I want to emphasize that she is in no danger. Provided, of course, that the French government complies with my demands."

The scene switched again. A hand-held ENG camera danced up to the VIP room. Adela Wheeler sat straight-backed and proud in her chair, her eyes downcast. The cameraman tapped on the glass door. She raised her head, and the camera caught her face, zoomed in on it, and held the shot.

"Yes," Smith said, "it is Mrs. Adela Wheeler, whom I dare say many among you will recognize as the mother of the American President. But to more pleasant considerations—for me, that is." The camera returned to Smith.

"As you see—and I assure you that nothing you have witnessed is faked—I and my associates are in complete command of this structure, in a way which I shall demonstrate in a moment. We shall retain control of the Eiffel Tower until I receive what I consider to be a fair ransom for it—and naturally, for the life of Mrs. Wheeler.

"I am given to understand that the tower cost in the region of one million, six hundred thousand US dollars to build. I have calculated that today's replacement value would be, say, sixty-eight million dollars.

"Therefore, I propose to return the tower to the people of France, in the same excellent order in which I found it, for the bargain price of thirty million dollars. That, I think you will agree, is not profiteering. The presence of Mrs. Wheeler should serve as sufficient—how shall I put it—inducement?"

Smith was clearly enjoying himself; Philpott sat dejectedly on the chaise longue, waiting for the knockout blow. The telephone rang, and Sonya sprang to answer it. "Give him a moment, please, Mr. Ambassador," she requested. "He wants to see the end of the Smith telecast."

Smith said, "Now observe closely. I want to show you why retaliation against me, the use of any force, military or civil, from the land or from the air, is completely useless."

Once more his face left the screen, and the exterior camera caught the outer edge of the tower, and rose dramatically towards the second gallery level. It found one of the Lap-Lasers, and halted. The evil black snout came into center-frame, and no one seeing it could doubt for a moment that it was a new and sophisticated weapon.

"What you are seeing now," Smith continued smoothly, "is one of four laser guns which guard the Eiffel Tower, its perimeter, and the immediate area. Also, naturally, the skies above it."

A curious double vocal effect began to creep in as the outside camera lingered on the Lap-Laser. Smith's message was being simultaneously piped through the tower's broadcast system. Monstrously amplified, it boomed out over the silent crowd. The ENG's sound camera picked it up and transmitted it, along with the clean feed from Smith's "studio."

From the telephone, Sonya said, "It's Richard Ravensberg. I've asked him to wait." Philpott signaled "message received." Smith's message was indeed being received, all over Paris, all over France, and in Belgium, Germany, and Luxembourg, all countries which can tune into French television channels.

"Let me tell you a little about these guns, or Lap-Lasers, as they are known," Smith went on. "I borrowed them, as it were, from the United States Army, who were testing them at a base near Stuttgart. They are possibly the most destructive weapons, on a small scale, ever devised. Of course, they cannot rival a hundred-megaton hydrogen bomb—but then nobody profits from the use of nuclear weapons. No—what the laser gun will do, fully armed as these are, is track and destroy, destroy utterly, anything entering the perimeter area of the Eiffel Tower, whether on the ground or in the air." Smith leaned forward, his expression solemn and concerned.

"I would advise the people gathered here, and the police, and the French Army, not to attempt to challenge these weapons, which are operating now on the face of the tower. That is all I have to say for the moment. I shall broadcast again in one hour. Au revoir."

The screen blanked out, and in government offices, in bars, homes, and shops throughout Paris, the reaction was one of numbed, fearful, enormous shock.

In Washington and London, Moscow and Peking, Cairo and Brussels, presidents and reporters scanned incoming telexes and panic-stricken diplomatic cables with mounting incredulity.

Philpott raced to the phone. "Roger," he rapped, "did you see it? All of it? Good. Now what I want you to do is this: I know Smith—his methods, his persona. I've studied him. Also I know a lot about these Lap-Lasers—because they're the really important factor, you realize? Without the lasers there, we might have a chance, although obviously we couldn't risk Adela's life. But with Smith in possession of the lasers, the authorities are—*completely*— *totally—powerless.* Clear?

"OK. Well, it's just possible my people and I may be able to tip the balance. Strictly for your ears alone—and I mean this, Roger . . . it must go no further. Your word? Done. Well . . . I have two operatives on the inside—in the tower. Now I want you to fix it with the French Government—and you must know by now that I have Giscard's Red priority, anyway—fix it for Sonya and me and UNACO to get in on the act. Like now. OK? Good. Call me back." He slammed the receiver down, and said to Sonya, "We wait."

Less than a minute later, the telephone rang again. Philpott snatched it up and said, "Roger? Who? Oh . . . oh, I see. No, of course. I'll hold." He looked at Sonya and shook his head, slowly, but not in defeat; in sympathy.

Then he put the receiver to his ear once more. "Yes, Mr. President," he said. "It's Malcolm. I know, sir, I know . . . I hope to give us an edge. Of course, of course—anything that could possibly cause even a hint of danger to Mrs. Wheeler is clearly out of the question.

"No, sir, no," he went on, "you have my absolute promise on that. Sure, I'll calm things down, and I'll be honored to act as your personal representative, interpreting your wishes. Please don't worry about that, Mr. President. And —Warren. Have faith. OK, I'll keep in touch." He cradled the machine, and it rang again almost at once.

It was the American Ambassador. UNACO were more than acceptable to the incident team, Ravensberg said. In fact—Philpott could consider himself as being virtually in charge of the operation. "And Malcolm—make sure the right side wins. The world is watching us—and the President considers Smith to be an appalling threat to international security."

At last Philpott smiled, albeit ruefully. Then he snapped into action. "Come on," he said to Sonya. "First stop, the French Ministry of the Interior. We have a hell of a lot to do. Hope to hell we're in time."

Whatever the spectacle, people have the sometimes dangerous habit of pushing small children to the front of a crowd, so that they can get a full view of the proceedings. The Eiffel Tower crowd was no exception.

A little girl of perhaps seven, blond hair caught up in bunches and held with ribbon, stood between two policemen, open-mouthed, clutching a large checkered ball.

Her mother held her by the shoulder, but her own attention was fixed unswervingly on the tower, even though she could see nothing that mattered. The child, from sudden, frustrated boredom, bounced the ball and failed to catch it. Worse, in her attempt to hold on to it, she hit it with her knee, and it rolled out across the road . . . and trickled towards the chalk-marked perimeter area of the tower.

With an annoyed squeal, the girl broke from her mother's grasp and ran for the ball.

Her mother screamed, and started after the child, but the police cordon held her in check. Some twenty feet along the fringe of the straining mass of people, a burly young man swept a policeman aside and streaked frantically in the wake of the little girl.

On the tower, a Lap-Laser moved fractionally to the left. The mouse-ear antennae pricked up, then started tracking the running figures. The computer picked the smaller target first, and the generator trucks beneath the tower sent power surging into the gun.

The running man dived just as the child reached her obstinately trickling toy. He scooped her up inches short of the chalk line, whose delineation had been dictated by Smith.

The ball rolled over the line. The laser gun moved at lightning speed. Its tube gleamed brilliant white. The outline of the ball glowed incandescently . . . and there was nothing. The ball simply disappeared. All that was left to show where it had been was a puff of smoke curling up from the tarmac.

The little girl's mother clutched her fiercely to her body, sobbing and rocking the child. There was total silence in the crowd around her. They stared at the smoke whiff in stunned, unbelieving horror.

Their limousine pulled up at the French Interior Ministry, and Philpott and Sonya got out and ran inside. Still the most notable feature of the skyline was the implacable giraffe of the Eiffel Tower.

Without ceremony, they were taken straight to the lofty conference room, where Guillaume Ducret, the Minister, was meeting representatives of the police, Army, and Civil Defense forces. Ducret held out his hand in manifest relief and said, "Mr. Philpott. I can't tell you how glad I am to see you." He introduced them all around.

Ducret, a handsome and aristocratic French politician of the Giscard-Malraux school, started to quiz Philpott when the door burst open again, and Police Commissioner August Poupon threw himself through it. He was all nervous energy, Poupon, but effective in a crisis. He was followed in quick order by Roger Ravensberg, trailing a brace of four-star US Army generals—Holmwood and Hornbecker—plus aides, and then by French military and industrial chiefs.

General Hornbecker and General Jaubert fell to discussing who could cause the most earth-shattering cataclysm in the shortest time. Jaubert declared, "I have a squadron of Mirage bombers in the air right now. They could be on the way in seconds."

Hornbecker replied, scornfully, "The Lap-Lasers will take them out in seconds! Now we would pick the lasers off with some very special missiles we have. . . ."

"Which would blow the Eiffel Tower, and Mrs. Wheeler, and half of Paris sky-high," Philpott put in cuttingly. "No, gentlemen. Monsieur Ducret and I have been placed in command of this operation. If we need your assistance, we will call on it; and we probably shall—but on our terms. Until we do, I shall be obliged if, unless you have anything truly helpful to contribute, you remain silent." It was rough, but effective: in the last analysis, the only way to treat generals.

Ducret coughed, and broke the embarrassed silence. Jaubert and Hornbecker, united at last, glared their collective loathing at Philpott. Ducret said, "May I suggest that our priority should be to learn all we can about the man who has committed this monstrous crime—the criminal who calls himself Mister Smith. Mr. Philpott? You can help us there, I believe."

Philpott cleared his throat and frowned. "Smith is one of the world's most extraordinary criminals, that's true, Minister," he said. "He's fantastically rich, but he has this dreadful urge . . . compulsion, to commit outlandish crimes. Freudian, possibly, but I believe he gets his kicks that way. No interest in politics or people; only crime . . . exalts him. So every year or so, he organizes a complex, brilliant, and normally successful criminal operation. He seems to be invulnerable. He thinks he is, anyway, which could be even more dangerous."

Ducret inquired, "Do we know anything that we are sure he's been responsible for?"

Philpott turned to Sonya. "Mrs. Kolchinsky? She—she will tell you, gentlemen. She has the facts."

Sonya itemized Smith's catalog of atrocity. "It was he," she said, "who stole sixty kilos of fission-grade Uranium U-235 from the Nuclear Fuel Fabrication plant at Blythe, Wyoming, in 1963. You remember? He held San Diego successfully to ransom for ten million dollars? Twenty dead in the panic.

"Two. In 1976, he sold a load of stolen Russian hand weapons—super-advanced equipment from their experimental test ground in Nevyansk—to terrorists in Libya. They turned up all over the place. A hundred and fifty dead in Manchester, England; two hundred in Tokyo; that airliner over Haifa; the Darmstadt massacre. Not Smith, I grant you—but Smith was the catalyst."

Sonya looked from face to face. "Do you want me to go on? The Channel Islands bank heist? Remember? Hell, he practically hijacked Jersey; commandos all over the island." She started to tick of another, but Ducret intervened. "No, Mrs. Kolchinsky, that will be enough, thank you. But why have I, any of us, never heard of a man like this? A man who actually lives in a Loire château, and apparently spends enormous sums of money here in my country."

Philpott explained. "He always disguises his identity. I hate to use the phrase, but he is a master of disguise. He can change his appearance so completely that his closest associates will fail to recognize him. Five years ago in Tokyo he appeared as a German: he speaks God knows how many languages. He was a Spaniard in Johannesburg two years back. But the main point about him, which I feel you have yet failed to appreciate, is that whatever identity he assumes, when Smith issues a demand, it is axiomatic that he will make it as difficult as possible to avoid compliance."

"You're saying he will give us no room to maneuver," Ravensberg put in.

"Exactly," Philpott replied. "Absolutely none. However, we've managed to make some room for ourselves. Gentlemen," Philpott sighed heavily, "there is no time for me to extract promises from you not to broadcast around what I'm going to tell you, so I'll trust that you won't. My organization, UNACO, has planted two agents in Smith's team on the Eiffel Tower."

The response was gratifying, although muted by the realization that, as Philpott said, "Whatever advantage it gives us, we can't capitalize on it for the moment, because we're out of touch with our people. So, not to gloss over the matter, we still know damnably little about what's going on up there." He pointed out the window at the tower.

Mike Graham looked keenly at the group gathered around him in the kitchen. Sabrina's special talent made her the leader; the other three commandos were lightweight, but would obey orders. A plan of the tower lay before them on the table, held down incongruously by four bulky explosive charges.

Graham's finger jabbed at the plan. "Here, here, here, and here—the stress points. That's where I calculate the tower is at its weakest—the fulcrums, so to speak. Hit them—and whoompf." He spread his hands wide, palm downwards. "No more Eiffel Tower."

"At each point?" Sabrina asked. "A full charge?"

Mike nodded. "Uh-huh. A twenty-five pounder." He picked up a detonator from a steel box. "And one of these. This is a radio-activated detonator. It's completely safe until activated by a radio signal. But once the command to arm has been delivered, it cannot be countermanded. However long the fuse duration is—that's the time you've got to get clear. If you can."

As it happened two of the commandos weren't even good ballast; they were scared stiff of heights. Tote contemptuously elbowed one out of the way and roughly hauled the other from the harness perched on the gallery rail. He took the quaking man's place, jumped down the side of the tower, and fitted two charges of molded explosive. Sabrina and the third commando did the others. Like Tote, she scorned the use of the restraining harness.

She worked, as always, quickly and with a seemingly inborn skill, swinging surely out on the angled iron struts, taping the rolls of pliable greyish-pink plastique into the girder beds, and pressing home the detonators. At the end of it, the bombs, mocking the innocence of their classroom plasticine substance, sat snugly like sinister bird's nests in the branches of the tower.

Sabrina flashed the uneasy commando above her a grateful smile. He may be scared, she thought, but at least he's competent. The commando offered her a hand to help her up, but she waved it impatiently away. "Look afer yourself," she instructed, "you're in more danger than I am."

The man shrugged, and balanced nonchalantly astride a cross-beam intended to take him to the safety of the spiral staircase. He lunged for the guard rail—and missed. His scream rang out on the air as he swiveled on the beam and tried to hook his legs around it.

The iron cut into the backs of his knees, and the pain reflexes straightened his legs. With a second wild, throaty cry, he fell from the beam. His body cannoned off an angle strut, and passed Sabrina close enough for her to feel the wind of its passage and the agony of his despair.

She anchored herself securely to an upright, and shot out a rigid arm and hand to grasp his own flailing fingers. It fastened on his hand, nails digging into the flesh, the grip moving to enclose his wrist like an iron band. The wrench on her corded muscles as she took the full strain of his body almost dislocated her shoulder, but she gasped with the numbing pain and gritted her teeth, trying to control the ugly rasp of the breath forced from her heaving chest.

Tote, from the opposite side of the tower, shouted, "Hang on! Hold him!" What, Sabrina thought wildly, does he think I'm trying to do?

"Get your feet on a girder!" she screamed, as the squirming man on the end of her arm kicked aimlessly out into space. Even Sabrina's strength was fast giving out, and she knew it would be only a matter of seconds before she must release him or join him in his death fall.

"For Christ's sake, I can't hold you!" she yelled. The girder she was clinging to bit into her muscles and sent waves of pain coursing through her body. Her fingers started to slip from the ironwork, her toes curled to ease the intolerable pressure, and she felt herself bowing and slumping down the beam. A sobbing moan of terror and frustration escaped from her clenched teeth.

Then it was over. The tension relaxed so suddenly as Tote, from below, swung across to catch the commando in a crushing hug, that Sabrina almost let go of the upright. She caught herself in time, and her body snapped back to embrace the girder, spacing her legs and arms away from the metal edges that were denting and ridging her flesh.

She heaved herself gratefully up to the gallery, and lay on the floor, blinking back tears of relief, and at last breathing deeply and evenly. Tote dumped the commando unceremoniously next to her. She turned to the man. "You all right?" she whispered. Dumbly, he nodded. "Yeah, thanks," he replied. Then he gasped and retched as Tote's booted foot caught him in the side.

"I'll say you're all right," the Finn growled. "You one lucky sonofabitch, your hear me, man? Me, I'd have dropped you. You hear that?" He kicked the commando again. The man grunted and coughed a spray of blood.

"Worse t'ing you do," Tote continued remorselessly, "is you nearly kill her. You, we can do without. She's worth ten of you—a hundred. You hear? I ever see you again, I kick you off the—tower myself."

Beneath the tower, the area was all bustle and activity. The Larousse trucks formed a circle like settler's wagons against marauding Indians. Inside the enclosure, Claude and C.W. led a team unspooling massive lengths of cable from a truck, and transporting them to an underground chamber.

They clamped the cables on to the tower's main power line. Other members of the crew brought in several small cartons, which they stacked against the wall as company for a couple of beer barrels.

As before, the cable-linking was a nerveracking job, and when it was done, C.W. stepped back from the bench and mopped the sweat from his brow. He looked for a freshener, and his eye fell on the beer barrels. He loped over to them, hunkered down, put his mouth under the spigot, and turned the valve.

Nothing came from the nozzle but the hiss of compressed air. "Jeeze," C.W. complained, "there's an awful lot of bubbles in your beer, Claude." Claude whipped around and barked, "Don't touch that. If you want a drink, wait until you get upstairs."

C.W. rose to his feet and shrugged. The drink he could do without . . . but the knowledge that at least some of Smith's beer barrels were filled with oxygen might come in handy.

Not for the first time, the black man cudgeled his agile brain for some way of getting the priceless information he had off the tower and into Philpott's hands. Here, in the basement, on the ground, he was so close to safety. All he had to do was cut and run. Except, he thought ruefully, that Claude would blast his head off before he'd taken half a dozen steps. . . .

The activity at the Interior Ministry was more controlled now. Philpott and Ducret kept useless talk down to the minimum, and concentrated on getting the best scientific and military advice on how to deal with the lasers.

At one stage it seemed as if they might have achieved a breakthrough, when a tall, gangling, humorless French boffin came up with a startlingly obvious solution.

"The guns operate on light beams," he explained earnestly, "so all you have to do is reflect the—how you say? —death ray back at the Lap-Laser."

Philpott leapt to his feet. "Mirrors, by God!" he exploded. "That's it! Big mirrors! Catch the beam, and bend it back. Why didn't we think of that before?"

He set the scientific team to work, but they mournfully reported half an hour later that if the angle of refraction wasn't absolutely correct, the bouncing beam could shear off large sections of the Eiffel Tower and miss the lasers altogether.

"Can't you fix the angle of refraction and keep it fixed?" Philpott pleaded, desperately. "When you're running with a damned huge mirror?" the tall boffin moaned. "Or when all they have to do is alter the angle of the laser anyway, and you're in even deeper trouble than before?"

Philpott reluctantly conceded defeat. He scowled when Ravensberg, in some trepidation, reported that both Capital Hill and the Élysée Palace wanted action—fast. "Tell 'em they'll get it when I think it's time, and not before," Philpott snarled. "Tell Washington I'll save Mrs. Wheeler even if I have to pay Smith his thirty million bucks. Tell Paris I'll save their money even if I have to endanger Mrs. Wheeler's life. Above all, make it clear that I'm in command. Tell anyone you meet that I can be a real bastard if I'm crossed."

Ducret glanced across at him sympathetically. "You appreciate what's happening, my friend," he ventured. "Only too well," Philpott replied, "but tell me, anyway."

Ducret studied his exquisitely tidy hands. "From the French viewpoint," he said, "our president is delighted that you're in command, as you say, because you are an American, and if you fail it will be an American failure. If one girder of the Eiffel Tower falls, you and your country will be held to account. If one American dollar passes from our treasury to Mister Smith, it will be your fault, not ours."

Philpott nodded, gloomily. "It's the same on my side," he admitted. "Should anything happen to the President's mother, I have no doubt whatsoever that, despite my long-standing friendship with Warren Wheeler, my department will close down virtually overnight. I shall be lucky if I can get a job teaching woodwork in a ghetto high school."

"What will you do, then?"

"Politically? Play one off against the other until I get what I want. When you're part of the United Nations, Ducret, you get used to walking on razorblades. With me, it's a way of life. But I normally do get what I want."

"And what is that?"

"Smith," Philpott replied unhesitatingly. "That's what I want—Smith. I want to take him out, Ducret. And by God I will."

"You're willing to stake your department, your career, on it?" Ducret inquired.

"I am. Perhaps even my life."

Ducret sighed. "Then I can only hope that the decisions you make in the next few hours are the right ones."

Philpott grinned. "Or that I can persuade Giscard and Wheeler that they're the right ones," he mused.

So the scheming and counterscheming went on, and the hot line between the two Presidents, Warren G. Wheeler and Valéry Giscard D'Estaing, buzzed with traffic. Eventually, they were compelled to consider paying Smith off, though neither realized that they had been cunningly manipulated to this conclusion by Malcolm G. Philpott.

Marcel LeGrain, the Finance Minister, was called into the conference room. "Let me make my position quite clear from the outset," the burly, pugnacious ex-rugby football forward stated. "If you give in to this bandit, I shall resign and take the key of the treasury with me.

"You cannot, and you must not, encourage the forces of anarchy that threaten the very foundation of our economic well-being. I say we grind this Monsieur Smith into the ground like an insect." He demonstrated by gouging his heel deeply into the carpet. Ducret winced, and added, "Splendid, Marcel. And of course, none of us will over-look the fact that, apart from anything else, it is also election year."

Philpott chuckled, and LeGrain was about to frame a barbed response when an aide tactfully buttonholed Ducret and pointed to the TV screen. "Our newest star is about to go nova again," he said.

They clustered around the set. Smith graciously allowed a commercial to wind up, then removed RTF from service and brought in the tower.

He looked grim. "It is now," he announced, "1 P.M. If the thirty million dollars I have requested is not in my hands within twelve hours, I and my associates will leave the tower—under the protection of our laser-guns. Shortly thereafter, four simultaneous explosions will reduce the Eiffel Tower to a scrap heap.

"I am sure," Smith continued, "that you would not wish that to happen. I am equally convinced that President Wheeler will not relish the thought that his mother will be in the tower when it goes up—because she will not, I regret to say, be accompanying us."

Smith allowed a few moments for the information to sink in, then produced an emotive trump card. "But why not let the lady speak for herself?" he suggested. The camera panned slowly to the left. Adela Wheeler sat at Smith's side.

"Do you expect me to plead for you, Mister Smith? Or for my life?" she demanded, bitingly.

"It is of small concern to me what you do, Mrs. Wheeler," Smith replied, and walked out of camera range.

Adela Wheeler turned to face the camera. No American watching her could fail to have swelled with pride. She might have been a frontierswoman daring Geronimo or Santa Anna to do their worst. To Philpott, she seemed like the Statue of Liberty come to life.

"That is a silly, greedy man," Mrs. Wheeler sneered. "If anyone out there wishes to ransom the Eiffel Tower, then that is their business. But do not, I beg you, take my presence here into account. Like the Eiffel Tower, I have been around a long time. It could be that both of us have outlived our usefulness.

"That I should join this extraordinary tower on the auction block to satisfy a lunatic megalomaniac at my time of life is unthinkable—obscene. Do not give in to him. Destroy him. His kind are not fit to breathe the same air as we do. If you want to part with your hard-earned francs, then send it to the International Children's Relief Fund. They need it. Smith doesn't."

Ravensberg jumped to his feet. "That's my girl!" he chanted. "Sock it to him, Adela, hot and strong." Ducret murmured, "Hear, hear—although I do not think Mister Smith will like it."

The camera came off Mrs. Wheeler and slid hurriedly back to Smith. His rage was barely controllable. "Whatever this gallant but foolish old woman says—you have twelve hours. That is all!"

CHAPTER
NINE

Smith prowled around the tower restaurant, frustration gnawing at his patience. This was the part of every operation that he loathed . . . the waiting game, while the fools on the other side debated how they could vanquish him and save their precious money.

He snorted in derision. If only they knew how little he cared about their money! He wanted only their pride and their willpower laid in shreds at his feet. He wanted them groveling, and acknowledging him as master. He desired the unsurpassable thrill of danger, and of victory. Defeat Mister Smith? The very notion was absurd! He had never been defeated. He never would be. He was truly invulnerable—the greatest brain in criminal history.

Smith sneered as he imagined the cohorts of politicians, generals, and policemen scheming assault after assault on the tower, then drawing back as they remembered the all-powerful lasers. The city officials would announce grandly that they had the solution: cut off the electricity supply, and render the lasers harmless.

Then they would hear the constant, jeering rumble of his generator trucks, and realize that he didn't need their power—he had his own. Smith chuckled. Someone might even come up with the ridiculous suggestion that you could reflect the laser beams with mirrors. Let them try, he thought. It would be the grandest firework display of all.

He poured himself a cognac, drank it at a gulp, and motioned to Claude. "It's time we took some more—

ummm—precautionary measures, I think? What do you say, Claude?" Claude glanced at the top team and the other commandos draped around the room, dozing, playing cards, or chatting desultorily. "The guns?" he queried. Smith nodded. "Tactfully, Claude, tactfully."

Claude made the diplomatic announcement: all personnel to report to the command post, with their weapons. Smith was there to receive his forces.

"I dislike bloodshed," he began, pompously, "and most of all, I abhor unnecessary accidents. While you are armed, but not conspicuously alert, accidents could occur leading perhaps to bloodshed. I propose to remove the risk by requisitioning your weapons."

There was a murmur of alarm from the group; Tote, particularly, did not favor the idea. Graham and C.W. looked immensely suspicious, and smelled a giant-sized rat. But, one by one, under the watchful gaze of Smith, and the cradled guns of Claude and Leah, they complied.

"Could this also imply a certain lack of trust?" Sabrina asked, as she filed past the dais and surrendered her AK 47 automatic rifle and MA 28 Meisner machine pistol. "Not at all, my dear," Smith assured her, "what absolute nonsense. It's merely, as I said, to avoid the possibility of errors."

Graham said, pointedly, "Are you and Claude and Leah going to avoid the possibility of errors happening too, Mister Smith?"

Smith looked at him sharply. "Someone has to be armed, Mike," he replied. "Naturally, it will be myself and my closest associates."

Graham and C.W. were on the point of launching a combined protest, when the telephone rang. Pei picked it up, and waved excitedly to Smith. "It is the Minister of the Interior, Monsieur Ducret, sir."

Smith grinned smugly. "As I forecast," he said. "A little ahead of time, but they have come to their senses." He crossed to the phone.

Ducret made it plain that he was not in the mood to haggle over Smith's demands. "Excellent," Smith purred. "Neither am I. What, then, can I do for you, Minister?"

Ducret cleared his throat. "The Finance Minister," he said, "tells me that to amass and count the staggering sum you require cannot be accomplished in the time you have allowed us. He requests that you extend the deadline until 10 A.M. tomorrow."

Smith's complacent smile slipped away. "That is out of the question," he declared flatly. "We shall leave the tower and detonate the explosives at precisely one o'clock in the morning, unless by that time I have thirty million dollars, in unmarked bills, in my hands. When you get the money, and not before, contact me again, and I will arrange a safety procedure for the men bringing it to the tower. That will not, by the way, involve immobilizing my laser guns."

The conversation was being relayed on loudspeakers throughout the Ministry conference room. Ducret raised his eyebrows to Philpott and Poupon, who were now the prime movers on their side. Philpott scribbled furiously on a pad, and handed the note to Poupon, who passed it to Ducret.

The Ministetr continued, "I'm afraid it simply is not possible, Mister Smith. You're a highly intelligent man, and I am sure you must appreciate that the task is beyond us. However, I have been authorized to offer you half the sum, fifteen million dollars, by ten o'clock this evening. That's all the US currency we have in the country, as far as we can trace. The rest we're getting from Switzerland and Luxembourg—but it takes time."

There was a pause from the tower; then Smith conceded the point. "Very well, Ducret," he said, "fifteen million dollars by ten o'clock tonight. But I am not giving you a further twelve hours to get the rest. You must place it in my hands by 4 A.M. at the latest. That is my final concession. Agreed?"

Ducret replied, "A moment, Mister Smith. I'll put you on hold. I must confer with my colleagues."

He looked at Philpott. "Well? Why is time so urgent to him? And what do I say now?"

Philpott guessed aloud that Smith wished to be paid before daylight; or perhaps his generators were due to run out at dawn, or thereabouts. Then a thought struck him. "Of course, there's one thing we haven't discussed generally, although Commissioner Poupon and I have considered it."

"And what is that?"

"How in God's name Smith plans to get safely off the tower once he has the ransom, and the lasers are presumably switched off."

Ducret considered the point. "If you have no ideas," he confessed, "then neither have I. So I suppose we have little choice but to agree."

He reopened the tower line. "I am waiting, Monsieur Ducret," Smith said acidly, "but my patience is not inexhaustible. Do I get what I want?"

Ducret replied, "Yes, Mister Smith. You do." And he put down the phone.

Sabrina wandered by the railed gallery, seeking a breath of fresh air. Graham approached her from the opposite direction, and they leaned on the rail together. He lit a cigarette, and said to her, quietly, "You're extremely elegant for a thief, Sabrina."

Sabrina's heart pumped; was he still teasing her? Was the crunch coming now? While it was still not too late for Smith to dispose of her—but leaving no chance for her to contact Philpott?

She forced herself to smile—languidly, she hoped. "Why, thank you, Mike," she said lightly. "Of course, it's not my only hobby."

Graham grinned. "I'm sure it isn't," he said. He smoked lazily, and they both looked out over the city. "Funny thing," he drawled, "I—uh—" the words trailed off.

"You what, Mike?" she asked.

"Oh—just one of those feelings. I've had it ever since we met, and I can't shake it."

"What is it?" Careful, she thought, careful; play it for all you're worth.

Graham looked at her, smiling. "I just believe I've seen you before, somewhere," he drawled, "some time or other. Simple as that. Nothing serious—huh?"

"No, no," she said a little too quickly, trying to keep her voice steady. "It's entirely possible that you have seen me before—although I honestly don't think we've met. But you see, once upon a time I was a model, a cover girl, that sort of thing. My picture got around a bit. It was all very boring."

There was silence from Graham. He drew deeply on his cigarette, then blew out the smoke in his lungs and admitted, "Yeah, that could be it. A bit dangerous for you, though, I'd have thought, getting your face on the front of *Vogue*."

She nodded enthusiastically. "It was. That was why I gave it up."

He said, "Oh, sure. I agree that we can't have actually met." He looked at her, his eyes shrewdly appraising. "I certainly would never forget a gorgeous chick like you if we'd even said hello, let alone held hands."

Sabrina flushed. "Thank you, kind sir," she simpered. Graham's eyes held her own; then his gaze moved out again and he sprang to alertness.

"Hey," he whispered, pointing to the park beyond the tower perimeter, "looks like the marines have landed."

She followed his finger. Military vehicles were jockeying into position, and impressive numbers of well-armed foot soldiers poured out of them.

Sabrina said, "Is it serious, d'you think?"

Mike shook his head. "I don't think so," he replied, and after a moment added, "let's see if we're still repelling boarders."

He flicked the cigarette far out on to the cool breeze. It traveled about ten yards, and started to spiral earthwards, when there was a brilliant white flash from above. The cigarette incinerated.

Claude had crept up softly behind them; he was an inveterate eavesdropper. He touched Graham on the shoulder, and Mike spun around. "You should watch your smoking," the scar-faced Frenchman advised. "It could be bad for your health."

As the sun started to sink, bathing the tower in a rosy haze, the military activity in the park of the Palais de Chaillot skirting the tower intensified. In the intervening hours, a low barrier had been erected most of the way around the tower. It marked precisely the thousand meter line from the center of the tower, and it was all the generals could think of doing.

They had established a No-man's-land between the barrier and the line of troops and military trucks—a gap of about a hundred feet. The only vehicle inside the no-go area was a police communications van.

The van had been rigged up as a complete communications center, putting Philpott and Commissioner Poupon in constant touch with anyone they wished—including the tower and the President of the United States. The transfer of the command post had been Philpott's idea. Fed up with inactivity, he had decided to come marginally out into the open, and convey somehow to Sabrina and C.W. that an urgent contact was needed.

"It was Smith who supplied the motive power," he explained to Poupon. "That crack he made about a safety procedure for the people bringing the money up to the tower. I had assumed, obviously, that the people in the tower must have some sort of protective machinery, otherwise the lasers would find them and burn them whenever they so much as came near the railing.

"Smith confirmed it. So I must assume that C.W., in particular, will try to get away, or at least make contact with us. If he's safe, C.W. can get down that tower in two minutes flat, and avoid ending up like they did—" He gestured towards the corpses of birds, literally fried, which had flown within the arc of the deadly lasers.

"But surely," Poupon objected, "they'll shoot him from the tower."

Philpott grinned crookedly. "Not unless the lasers are turned off," he said. "They can gobble up bullets just as easily as birds. And Smith doesn't dare kill the lasers. We'd be in there like a shot if he did."

Poupon nodded. "Of course. Well, it's a chance, even if it's a slim one. But as you say, it's better than sitting on one's derrière at the Ministry, hein?"

Philpott chuckled, and added, "Don't expect anything until sundown. C.W. will want the cover of darkness, even though he doesn't need as much of it as Sabrina would."

Poupon was mystified. "Why ever not?" he asked.

Philpott chuckled again. "He's as black as the ace of spades," he replied. "In fact—but for God's sake don't tell him I said so—in many ways C. W. Whitlock *is* the ace of spades."

A senior police officer knocked respectfully on the door of the van, and ushered in a superintendent from the Paris

City Engineer's department. Soon, all three were pouring over detailed plans of the Eiffel Tower.

The sun set, reluctantly it seemed, and as the last golden fingers of light caught the tower, a dark shadow moved behind a staircase linking two sections of spidery, criss-cross ironwork, far up the side of the structure. A sound, of some object dropping and striking the frame, echoed faintly, and C.W. froze to the girders.

At the communications van, Sonya, Philpott, and Poupon took advantage of the remaining light to train binoculars on the tower. "Any luck?" Philpott grunted. "Nothing," Sonya replied. "There are miles of ironwork there. It's like—well, you know."

"I know," Philpott sighed. "The light'll be gone in a few moments," Poupon chipped in helpfully.

"Thanks a million," Philpott said sourly. He concentrated on scanning the tower, and muttered, "Come on C.W., come on baby."

The black man felt it was safe to move again. He swung out and shimmied across the frame until he was pressed against the girders facing Philpott's van. He had long since spotted Philpott, although neither he nor Sabrina had needed any prompting to make contact. The trick had been getting away from the restaurant and the ever-vigilant Claude. C.W. had pleaded a call of nature, and slipped through the toilet window. It had been as easy as hanging off an iron tower from your fingertips.

Now he unclipped the metal tag on his chest, and held it out in front of him. There was still the odd ray of sunlight streaming through the gathering clouds, and C.W. twisted the metal strip back and forwards, this way and that, praying that a light beam would strike the tag.

Sonya spotted the brief flash, and screamed out, "There it is! Just below the second landing. A flash of light! C.W.'s signaling to us. I can even see him, just about."

Philpott and Poupon swiveled their binoculars. "Where?" Philpott demanded. "Opposite that little staircase, right by the support beam," Sonya pointed.

"Got him," Philpott breathed. Then, "Jesus Christ, he's using sign language. Sonya, get a pad!" C.W.'s fingers moved with amazing dexterity, and Philpott translated just as fluently.

"Take this down," he ordered. ". . . incredible—security —precautions . . . shit, missed that one. Wait . . . Mrs. Wheeler—OK—so—far. All—personnel—disarmed—except—Smith—and—lieutenants."

The light had held long enough for C.W. to complete his report. Sonya read it out breathlessly: "Smith hasn't told us escape plan, but training included everything from aqualungs to high wire. Also they have six-berth helicopter at Château Clérignault, in Loire—" she stopped.

"What next?" Philpott demanded.

"Nothing," Sonya replied, "that's all. It ended there."

Philpott rubbed his jaw. "A bit abruptly," he mused. "Could anything have happened to C.W.?"

A hand clamped over C.W.'s mouth and jerked him back into the shadows behind a grider. Graham whispered into his ear, "Don't make a sound."

C.W.'s eyes snapped upwards. Claude was descending the staircase, a torch in his hand. He paused within feet of C.W. and Graham, and stared fixedly out at the communications van. The light had failed totally now, and Claude whistled under his breath. He shrugged, and climbed back up the staircase to the second level, and took the elevator down to the restaurant. He was still troubled by C.W.'s absence, and it occurred to him that he had not seen Mike Graham, either, in the past ten minutes or so. Or Sabrina Carver.

Mike eased his hand off C.W.'s mouth and hissed, "Your fairy godmother has just saved your hide." At that instant, a vicious judo chop landed on the side of his neck. He grunted and staggered, his knees buckled, and Sabrina, standing over him, prepared to chop him again.

C.W. caught her descending hand. "Not him! He just saved my life."

Sabrina breathed out. "So, you're even, because you've just saved his."

Graham rubbed his neck ruefully and remarked, "You're a lot tougher now than you were the first time we met. That unarmed combat course you took after I left must have taught you a hell of a lot."

"So you *did* recognize me," she gasped. Mike grinned amiably. "Once seen, baby . . ." he said. "Could I forget a form like yours?" Sabrina sulked.

"And whose side are you on these days, Mike?" C.W. inquired.

"Mine," Graham replied, "and the CIA's. Undercover. Effectively, I've been working with you."

"Then why have you been such a miserable, moody . . ." Sabrina burst out.

"So that, if the pair of you goofed, and got yourselves dead, you wouldn't take me with you," Graham returned. He asked if Philpott had been able to reply to C.W.'s message, and the UNACO agent explained that there had been no time.

"Pity," Mike said. "We'll have to go it alone, then."

"You have a plan?" Sabrina asked.

"Sort of," Mike answered. "We'll have to play it by ear . . . ad lib, if you get my meaning. I'll tell you what I've got in mind, and then we'd better beat it back to the restaurant by separate routes before Claude goes bananas."

Apart from a suspicious glare from Claude—who, fortunately, had not confided his uneasiness to Smith—their return to the first landing aroused no interest. They drifted in one by one, Graham to resume a hand of cards with Tote and Pei, Sabrina to chat with two pretty Japanese girls who, for Red Army commandos, were well up in Western fashion trends. C.W. slumped in an armchair, feigning sleep. Half an hour passed, during which Smith talked briefly with Claude and Leah, and left the room. Ten minutes later, C.W. dragged himself to his feet and announced he was going off to find something that more closely resembled a bed. Nobody appeared to mind.

C.W. took the elevator up, and passed the routine second landing gallery patrol of two men, disarmed now but still under orders to be watchful and report regularly. C.W. calculated it would be three minutes before they reached that spot again.

The sentries returned on time: when you have nothing to do but walk around in circles, it becomes a matter of pride to do it well. As soon as they had passed, a coil of rope smuggled on to the tower by C.W. in a cold box snaked down from above, and dropped clear to the first level. The rope lay in the hollow of a box girder and, but for the projection of the rail, which it loosely rounded, would not be noticed by anyone from the tower—unless they were leaning out. C.W. shimmied down the rope, and glided past the landing to the primary level.

The first—and most important—part of Mike Graham's plan was to get Mrs. Wheeler off the tower. If that could be accomplished, they would only have fifteen million pounds of badly organized metal to worry about. C.W. hung suspended from the dark thread of the slim nylon rope, and inched his way down to the VIP room.

He drew level with the window. Mrs. Wheeler, as expected, was there, sitting grim-faced in her chair, staring directly across the room, away from the window. C.W. was on the point of tapping the glass to attract her attention, when she opened her mouth and spoke—apparently to no one.

Right on cue, Smith came into the picture, walking in the direction of the window—but looking at Mrs. Wheeler. C.W. froze and made to take himself and the rope out of sight. As he moved carefully across the face of the tower, Mrs. Wheeler's eyes shifted towards the window and locked on to C.W.'s. She gave not the slightest flicker of a response, but looked back at Smith, and held his gaze with hers.

"I wish I could convince you, Mrs. Wheeler," Smith was saying, "that a heartfelt appeal from you to the authorities would speed up the entire process, avoid possible bloodshed, even loss of life, and totally ensure your own freedom. I do not wish you to betray anyone, least of all yourself; merely to appear on television once again, or speak on the telephone."

Mrs. Wheeler drew herself up grandly. "I find the idea that I should plead for my life utterly repulsive, Mister Smith," she said. "I am a grandmother, I have brought up a man who is now President of the United States, and I will not demean myself by appearing to toady to a barbarian like you. If you want your money, you're going to have to get it without my help. That is my last word on the subject."

Smith replied, slyly, "I can be very insistent when I wish to be."

Adela Wheeler laughed, genuinely amused. "Thumbscrews?" she jeered. "The Iron Maiden, the Chinese boot, water torture? Perhaps the strappado? Really, Mister Smith, I'm too old and too obstinate for that sort of childish twaddle. Now run along and threaten someone your own age."

C.W. had braced himself against the girders to ease the pressure on his arms. His hold on the rope relaxed. What he had not reckoned on was that the wind would pick up —had, indeed, been threatening to do so since sundown, but he had been too preoccupied to notice. The rope was caught by a gust, and flapped against the external metal wall of the room.

Smith's head whipped around, like a striking snake's. Quickly Adela Wheeler boomed, in her most formidable voice, "Mister Smith! I have asked you to leave. Surely even a prisoner has the right not to be bored by her jailer. Now please go! We have no more to say to each other."

Smith evidently decided that the noise outside meant nothing. He returned Mrs. Wheeler's challenging stare, and gave her a mocking bow. "Madame," he said, courteously, "I can well see how you came to be the mother of a great president—and how President Wheeler came to be the man he is. For the moment, goodbye." He wheeled and left the room, locking the door behind him. Mrs. Wheeler remained motionless for a long, long two minutes, hoping that the man outside the window would do the same.

Her innately suspicious mind reaped its reward. Smith crept noiselessly back to the room, and peered through the glass panel—first at Mrs. Wheeler, then at the window. Adela felt his gaze burning into her, but did not deign to acknowledge him. She leaned back in her chair, composed her interlinked fingers on her lap, and closed her eyes. Smith's never left the window. For another full minute and a half he stood there. Then, satisfied, he walked away.

C.W., who had been on the point of swinging back to contact Mrs. Wheeler, saw Smith's face reflected in a vanity mirror hanging on the wall behind her chair. He jerked the rope tight, and pressed himself into the ironwork until he felt he was becoming part of the fabric of the tower. It was excruciating, but it worked.

Adela breathed a sigh, and swiftly crossed to the window and opened it. "It's all right," she called. "The wretched man is gone." C.W. hoisted himself on to the windowsill, tucked the rope back into the girder, and climbed into the VIP room.

* * *

The iron staircase, which spiraled at intervals, and broke on to platform landings of its own, actually connected the first and second levels of the tower. Claude, restless as always, and not being able to locate the supposedly sleeping black commando, had taken the elevator once more to the second level to check on things up there. He had his Kalashnikov slung over his shoulder.

He walked around the gallery, met and chatted with the patrol, and told them, unnecessarily, to keep their eyes peeled. When they left to resume their beat, Claude stepped to the rail and peered over. All was in darkness but for the lights from the first level, and the arc lamps mounted on poles at the sizeable military encampment across in the palace gardens. The crowd appeared at last to have drifted away. The thousand-meter perimeter at that point was now marked by a series of road lamps and a hastily contrived electric fence, guarded by lines of police.

Claude grinned, and experienced a feeling of great well-being. His composure shattered when he heard the distinct slap of C.W.'s rope, caught once more by the rising wind, against the ironwork. Claude unslung his rifle, flipped off the safety catch, and cautiously descended the stairway.

Mike Graham sensed his coming, then heard it. Graham was himself on the stairs, halfway between levels. He slid off the steps and outside the frame of the tower, wishing he had a gun—a knife—anything. Claude passed him. Soundlessly, Mike crept back on to the iron platform.

Claude felt his way down the steps, cursing his lack of foresight in not bringing a torch. Then he saw the rope, quite clearly. It had slipped from its mooring, and was pulling away from and thudding back onto the girder, as the wind raced and moaned through the latticework of the tower. Claude stepped onto a cross-beam, and peered downwards. He thought he saw something at the end of the rope. He lifted his rifle, and sighted on it, his finger curling around the trigger.

Graham's full weight crashed down on his shoulders in a flying leap from the stairway. Claude screamed, and the rifle slipped from his grasp.

It struck a girder, and bounced off into the crisp night air on the still-rising breeze. From overhead, a Lap-Laser tracked it, glowed white, and sent a beam of blinding light after it. The Kalashnikov, metal and all, was reduced to ashes in half a second.

Claude rose savagely to his feet, and tackled the man who had dive-bombed him. They were matched for strength, and they clutched and fought in silence, to the howling of the wind.

Mike got a neck-hold on him, but the Frenchman suddenly relaxed his entire body. Mike's grip loosened momentarily and Claude wriggled free. He jumped down to the next platform, which linked with a catwalk taking a path across the tower to the head of the next stairway . . . the last flight before the restaurant level.

There, Claude turned on Graham and snarled his defiance. He adopted a *savate* stance, and beckoned to Mike. "Venez, venez," he hissed. "Come, little one. I will take you to pieces."

Mike reached the platform, but went no further. He had seen Claude demonstrate his skill at French foot-fighting. At that, and at the Chinese martial arts, Claude was without peer in France.

He had to land but one vital kick, and he would send Graham hurtling down the tower to his death.

CHAPTER
TEN

On tiptoe, but with his feet well-spaced for balance, Claude advanced along the catwalk towards Graham. Mike was half-crouching, facing Claude sideways in a classic judo stance to present as small a target as possible. Claude stood ramrod straight, hands sloping downwards at thirty degrees from his body, fingers extended, his poise and strength going into the preparation needed for the jump-kick which is the hallmark of the *savate* fighter.

All the light they had was the dim glow from the first level, the moon, and the phosphorescent haze that every city throws up. The first stabbing kick came from nowhere, too fast for Mike even to sense, though he ducked in anticipation. It landed on the upper part of his right arm, and Graham left like he'd been injected with a jackhammer.

He hissed out his pain and leapt back on to the platform. The wind rose to mock him, whipping his hair over his eyes, and causing him to raise both arms as if he were fending off demons attacking him from every direction. But there was only one demon, and he was right in front of Graham, dancing in again, seeking for the one solid death kick that would put the contest beyond argument.

Mike nursed his right arm, knowing that he had been lucky the first time: Claude had tried for his belly, and Graham had unknowingly lurched too soon into a lower crouch.

Claude aimed next for the knee—the part of Graham

nearest to him as Mike resumed his defensive hunch. Claude folded his own wiry body into a question mark, left the catwalk nine inches under his feet, snapped his frame back almost to the horizontal, and lashed out.

This time Graham was ready. He guessed where Claude would strike, skipped to one side and threw himself forward, chopping down viciously with his hand at the Frenchman's extended leg.

But Claude's leg was no longer there. He had executed a mid-air pirouette, and was now shooting out his other deadly foot backwards. This kick, too, found its mark: on Graham's shin. But it lacked the power even of the first assault, and did no more than raise an ugly welt on the American's leg.

Claude twisted his body again and, like a gymnast, landed perfectly balanced in a crouch, heels together, arms outflung. Graham charged at him now in frustration and sheer rage, and aimed a kick at Claude's apparently unprotected body. Claude laughed, and threw himself into a backwards somersault on the catwalk—jogging into an upright striking stance.

Mike pounced once more—sure that his superior weight and reach must give him an irresistible momentum . . . it was the chance for which Claude had been waiting.

He crowed in delight, and left the metal floor in the kick that would be the coup-de-grâce, the terminal move in an unequal struggle.

And the realization of the terrible danger into which he was rushing pellmell, rampaged through Graham's brain and brought his headlong charge to a sudden, numbing halt. Claude had already embarked on the movement that was to guarantee him a crushing victory—a kick that would strike with appalling force at Mike's heart, killing him instantly, and sending his corpse tumbling through the spider's web of metal struts to break itself on the concrete far below.

His aim was precise, the strength he summoned into his leg was more than sufficient to deliver the death-blow—but he was three inches short. Graham just wasn't where his impetuous leap should have taken him.

Claude landed flat on his back, his hands taking most of the weight of the jarring fall. Stars swam before his eyes, and his next conscious feeling was of Graham descending on him like a maddened bear, no science or finesse, just a blind lunge that brought Mike where he most wanted to be—at close quarters with Claude, and out of reach of those damaging feet.

Mike's knees drove into Claude's stomach, and knocked the wind from him. Graham hauled the Frenchman to his feet, and smashed his fist into Claude's face. Claude staggered back into a stout cross-girder—then grabbed on to it with both hands, and grinned again as Mike stampeded within kicking distance.

But Claude had nothing like the perfect balance his craft demanded. The girder pressed into the small of his back, and he was almost seesawing on it, his head and upper torso well outside the frame of the tower as he aimed his right foot as far up Mike's body as he could get it.

Graham took the kick in the stomach almost with contempt—and Claude's armory counted suddenly for nothing. Mike jinked inside his other foot, and brute force took him into a wrestling crouch over Claude's body, now bent agonizingly back over the iron bar.

With studied deliberation, Graham reached out his free hand, and coolly ripped away from Claude's chest the electronic metal safety tag.

Claude had been expecting anything but that. His body froze, and all movement ceased in him as the moonlight fell on the weaving laser gun fifty feet above him. The mouse-ears searched out and found this unprotected foreign body in its territory, and sent a beam of blinding white light lancing through the Frenchman's heart.

In the restaurant, Smith was standing with Pei at the computer console. Pei reported that a Lap-Laser had fired. He used the evidence of his eyes: he had seen the series of glowing lights crossing the screen of the console—a sure sign that one of the guns had operated.

Smith scanned the console intently . . . it could have been a bird—or it might mean something infinitely more dangerous to him. Then for a second time the screen pulsed with light, registering the death of Claude Légère.

"There it is again!" Pei shouted. "It's fired twice."

"Give me the position," Smith ordered. "The exact position."

He strode from the little stage, fuming, to gather his closest lieutenants around him. He couldn't see Claude in the restaurant, and was hurrying out to the railed gallery when he almost collided with Leah coming in.

"Where is Claude?" Smith demanded. Leah replied that she thought Claude had been with Smith in the restaurant.

"If he was in there I wouldn't be asking for him!" Smith shouted. "Now if you can't be more helpful than that, call him on the bleeper."

Leah hurried to the radio, and sent out a signal which would activate Claude's personally coded communicator. There was a pause, and she signaled again. Smith paced over to the desk and pushed her roughly aside. He operated the keys himself.

"Why isn't he answering?" he gritted.

"Maybe . . ."

"Maybe what?"

"Maybe he—can't," Leah whispered.

Sabrina scuttled over the face of the tower like a human fly. A rope was looped around her body, and she dropped lightly on to the platform where she was to have met Graham, to see him dragging Claude's body back along the catwalk.

She gasped, "What's happened? Are you all right?"

Mike looked up, and whistled in relief. "Christ," he said, "you're a sight for sore eyes. I ran into trouble with Claude, and I had to administer a rather drastic remedy to stop him kicking me silly."

Sabrina looked at him questioningly, and Mike opened his hand and showed her the metal tag. She caught her breath, and shone her torch on Claude's face . . . then brought it slowly down his body. "Oh, my God," she said.

"Don't feel sorry for him," Mike whispered. "He was trying to kill me. Just help me get rid of him."

Sabrina said, "Where's C.W.?"

"Still in the VIP room with Mrs. Wheeler, I guess," Mike answered. "Why?"

Sabrina unslung the rope from her shapely frame. "Let's

send him a present." Mike grinned, and pinned the metal tag back on Claude's body. They tied the rope around his waist, balanced him once more on the cross-strut, and lowered him gently down the side of the tower. Mike peered at the splash of light coming from the window of the VIP room, and said, "A few more feet, perhaps." They paid out more line carefully, until Graham ordered, "Stop. That should just about do it."

Adela Wheeler's hand flew to her mouth when she caught sight of the dangling corpse. "Dear God," she cried, "what now?"

C.W.'s eyes darted to the window, and he said, "Oh, oh. Somebody's been having trouble."

He crossed the room and peered closer. "But nothing compared with the trouble poor old Claude's been having," he murmured. He gestured to Mrs. Wheeler. "Watch the door, sweetie. We have an uninvited guest." C.W. opened the window and hauled the body inside.

At that moment, Smith's voice echoed around the tower through the loudspeaker. "This is Mister Smith. All personnel come to the restaurant now."

Sabrina dropped the rope over the side, and she and Mike flattened themselves in the shadows of I-beams as the second level patrol scorned using the elevator, and clattered down the staircase to the first landing. After a suitable interval, Mike and Sabrina followed them.

The entire commando crew were lined up by Smith, and Sabrina and Graham made up the numbers. Smith did a quick head-count.

"Right," he snapped, "has anyone seen Claude Légère in the past fifteen minutes?" There were blank looks or shaking heads up and down the line.

"Or C.W.?" Again, negative. Smith's eyes darted from man to man, woman to woman. They rested longest on Graham and Sabrina.

"There is nowhere on this tower," he said slowly, "that they could possibly be, where they would have been unable to hear the announcement I made just now, and which all of you heard plainly. So, either they are off the tower —which is inconceivable—or something has happened to one, or the other, or both. I want them found. I want them found now."

Smith allocated various commandos to search appointed sectors of the tower, and directed his last command at Graham: they would go together to the VIP room to check on Mrs. Wheeler. Leah trailed dutifully in Graham's wake, and Sabrina, whose search area included the block where the VIP room lay, followed some distance behind. It meant circumnavigating the first level gallery, and they arrived to find Tote standing guard.

"Why did you not answer my summons?" Smith snapped. "And leave my post?" Tote queried, with a touch of studied insolence. Smith bristled, but chose to ignore both the insolence and the improper form of address. Privately, he admitted that his troops had become more and more informal the longer the operation lasted, and this tended to make him lose his iron control. Nonetheless, Tote had been correct to stay.

"Is everything all right, then?" he inquired. "Nobody's been near here," Tote grunted, "not while I've stood guard." Smith instructed him to unlock the door.

Adela Wheeler's chair was facing three-quarters to the window. They could see her hands folded in her lap, and the shapely ankles, and her feet in their high court shoes. Her face and hair were hidden, both enveloped in the big, soft cushion. She was clearly asleep, and, irrationally, this infuriated Smith.

"Stay by the door, Graham," Smith ordered. "Leah— wake her. I find the sight of her offensive."

Mike stood at the open door, hands clasped behind his back. His muscles clenched and his eyes widened as the door moved of its own volition, the handle coming to rest neatly in his hand. He pressed back tentatively on the door —and met solid resistance.

Leah could still not see Mrs. Wheeler's face. She said, "Are you awake?" When she got no response, she repeated, more loudly, "Mrs. Wheeler—are you awake, I said?"

She bent down slightly, and shook the velvet cushion. It dropped to the seat of the chair past the drooping figure's arms. With its support gone, the head lurched sideways—and Claude's dead, agony-filled eyes stared back at her.

Leah screamed, and screamed again. The sight of the corpse grotesquely dressed in the party gown, stockings

and fashionable shoes of an elderly woman completely un-
nerved her. Even Tote, at her shoulder, hissed and swore.

Smith rushed forward, beads of sweat starting along his
forehead. His eyes took in the body, and then flew to the
window. Leah screamed once more, and Smith struck her
with uncaring strength across the face with the back of his
hand.

"Now!" Graham hissed, and moved away from the door.

"Obliged, buddy," C.W. whispered. He and Mrs. Wheeler
—she now wore Claude's clothes, and shoes, and his metal
safety tag—slipped out of the room.

"Shut up, you fool," Smith shouted, and Leah subsided
to a whimper. Smith crossed to the window. Tote at his
elbow. Tote pointed, and Smith peered into the night.
There was a rope, running up to an I-beam. Smith jerked
the window open, and poked his head out. As far up the
tower as he could see, nothing was there that shoudn't have
been there. No movement, no telltale flash of light; he
strained his ears . . . no intrusive footsteps rang out on the
metal treads.

He turned back to Graham. Smith was sweating freely
now, and spittle started to form at the corners of his mouth.
His eyes ranged wildly from Leah to Graham to Tote, and
back down to Claude. It was simply not even remotely
possible that one of his projects could go wrong. "Do you
hear, whoever you are?" he muttered. "It is not possible."

Graham raised his eyebrows at Smith, and Smith's control snapped. "Search!" he screeched. "Search, damn you!
Search everywhere, everything!"

He turned on Tote, and grasped his shirt-front. "You
say no one came in, or out, while you were here?" Tote
nodded, dumbly. "Then how did she get out of the room?"
Smith asked, icily. Tote pointed towards the window.

"It's impossible," Leah said. "At her age? She isn't a
mountaineer, for God's sake."

"No, but C.W. is," Tote said. "He can climb anything,
up or down."

Smith swore, in a language he was confident none of
them recognized. He charged across the room to a sofa,
and ripped the cushions off. "There must be something
here, there must!" he shouted. He ran to a closet, pulled
open the door, and yanked out towels, tablecloths, and nap-

kins. The other three stood rooted to the spot as Smith lost
his cool. Then Leah went to him, and put her hand on his
arm. "Liebchen," she said, "stay calm. This is not you. Be
still, and think. We depend on you—only you."

The flattery was therapeutic. Smith breathed hard and
deeply, and slowly the fury left his eyes. He licked his lips,
and almost visibly pulled himself together, his chest rising
and settling, his shoulders squaring.

"You're right, Leah," he said, "this is no time for hys-
teria. We have to be methodical. They are still on the
tower. We shall find them. Graham, Tote . . . at the first
sight of Whitlock—kill him, instantly. I have no wish to
know for whom he is working. I want him dead.

"Do not, however," he cautioned, "make a mistake. Mrs.
Wheeler is presumably wearing Claude's clothing. In the
dark, she could be taken for the negro. Be careful. Now
go! And get help. Everyone is to search for them!"

Graham and Tote hurried from the room—Graham to
try to locate C.W.; Tote to link up with Pei, who had been
left on duty by the telephone. On the far side of the landing, a shadowy figure in battlegarb came out of the
shadows. Smith stopped in the doorway, and leveled his
machine-pistol.

"Who is that?" he demanded. "Advance, or I'll fire. The
lasers can't stop bullets here, as you must know."

Sabrina stepped into the light, holding a metal object
in her hand. "I don't know what's going on," she said, "but
I found this over there by the railing," she nodded her head
behind her. She offered the slim steel box to Smith. It was
Claude's communicator.

Graham had covered no more than three yards when
C.W.'s voice reached him from the shadow of an open
door next to the VIP room. "So what now?" C.W. said.

Mike turned on his heel, to see Smith and Leah engrossed in the examination of Claude's communicator, as
if it could speak to reveal some hidden secret of how the
Frenchman had met his death. "Come," Graham replied,
"and hurry."

C.W. and Adela Wheeler followed him, and Mike's body
effectively masked their return to the VIP room from the
group standing at the railing. Once inside, C.W. switched
off the light. Mike locked the door, and immediately re-

gretted it. It should have been locked from the inside, with
C.W. in charge of the key.

He made a second move towards the door, but Smith
strode suddenly from the railing to stand beside him.
"You've locked it?" he said. Mike nodded. "Good," Smith
remarked, pulling the key from the lock.

"We know for an absolute certainty that Mrs. Wheeler is
not in there," he said. "Every other inch of this tower will
be searched until we find her, even if you have to pull the
rivets apart with your bare hands."

Mike gulped and darted a sidelong glance at the VIP
room. "What are you waiting for?" Smith snarled. "Get on
with it."

Graham turned away in despair, and trotted back to the
restaurant. There was little he could do about it now, except hope to relieve Smith of the key later on.

Until then, C.W. and Adela Wheeler were trapped.

The President's mother and the black agent of UNACO
crouched behind the sofa that Smith had assaulted, away
from prying eyes at the glass door. "Do you have any
ideas, Mr. Whitlock?" Mrs. Wheeler asked gently.

"One," C.W. replied. "While we're still undisturbed, I'll
get in touch with my boss."

He swathed a three-quarter shield around the lightbulb,
and crossed to turn on the light. Just a chink of light from
the bulb was all that was visible . . . but it was pointing out
of the window. And C.W. knew that Philpott would be
watching for it.

Sonya Kolchinsky lay flat on top of the communications
van command center, trying to adjust to a more comfortable position. She took her weight on her elbows, and
fixed the binoculars to her eyes. She let out an exclamation,
and Philpott, from inside the van, shouted, "What is it?"

"A light flashing from the tower," she answered. "It
must be a code . . . yes, it is. And it's C.W."

Philpott and Poupon hurried out, and looked anxiously
up at her, "Well, what's he saying?" Philpott asked.

"Hang on . . ." Sonya replied, "he's repeating it. 'We—
have—a—new—recruit. Gray? No Graham.' It's Mike
Graham," Sonya burst out excitedly, "he's on our side
after all."

Philpott breathed a huge sigh of relief. "Then Sabrina's still OK," he grinned at Poupon, "and we've got a real team working in there. We can still win, Poupon old bean. We can still do it."

"There's more," Sonya said. " 'We—are—going—to—try—to—bring—Mrs.—Wheeler—out,' " she pronounced slowly. "He's going on: 'Can—you—arrange—diversion—now—question mark. Suggest—paying—first—half—of—ransom. Is—possible—question mark,' "

Philpott turned urgently to the Commissioner. "Is it possible? It's *got* to be. It might be the only chance we have of saving Mrs. Wheeler. And if anyone can get her off that damned tower, it's C.W. Make it possible, Poupon. Don't take no for an answer."

Poupon reached for the phone. "Do not worry, my friend," he assured Philpott. "When Poupon says 'jump,' they go up a long, long way. Allo, allo. Conference room? Get me the Finance Minister. I'll give you ten seconds."

Smith paced the restaurant floor, a walkie-talkie clasped in his fist, the riding crop (which someone had brought from the château) incongruously dangling from the other hand. Smith seemed to draw comfort from it, and occasionally lashed a tabletop or chair-back. Graham was receiving a phone report, and Sabrina and Leah Fischer manned walkie-talkies, making notes on memo pads.

"Has anyone found anything?" Smith asked querulously. Mike shook his head; Leah lifted her finger from the communicator button, and did likewise.

"How could C.W. have slipped through all our checks?" Smith mused, agitatedly. "He's a thief, an international thief—a master criminal. Who could he be working for? Who could possibly pay him more than I'm paying him? Unless—"

"Unless what?" Leah said.

"Unless he's not C. W. Whitlock, but some other black," Smith supplied.

"No," Leah stated, positively. "Fingerprints, voice-print, pictures . . . everything checked. I don't know why he's doing what he's doing, but he's Whitlock. I'd bet my life on it."

Smith grinned, evilly. "You may yet find that you have,

Leah. Whitlock was willing to take the chance when Graham made the same arrangement with him over the Lap-Laser tag. Shall we find a test for you to take, my dear?"

Leah felt the blood drain from her face. She, and not Smith, had okayed all five new members of the team. The computer had been specific: they were whom they claimed to be . . . but the computer could not read their minds. What if any of them—all of them—were agents of some intelligence power, as well as the criminals they were clearly identified as being? It was a frightening thought, and she dismissed it.

"You know you can rely on me, sir," she whispered huskily. "I have never let you down, have I? Ever?"

Smith shook his head. "But those who serve me, Leah, can afford only one mistake," he replied. "You might have made yours. We shall see. We shall see."

He stepped down from the little platform on to the floor of the restaurant, walking casually from Leah to Sabrina, Sabrina to Graham, Graham to Leah—to Sabrina.

"You were—how shall I put it?—friendly with C.W., were you not, Sabrina? Perhaps a little—too 'friendly.' Would you think too friendly, my sweet?" He touched her face gently, caressing her with the thong of the riding crop, trailing the leather loop down her cheek, across her mouth, up her other cheek, then tracing the straight line of her nose, and coming to rest in the dimple of her chin.

It was a disturbing experience. Sabrina was mesmerized, like a rabbit trapped in the coruscating jewels of a snake's eyes. She breathed, "Please don't touch me like that. I have done nothing to betray you. You have my word."

Smith drew the whip away. The girl's lips parted, and the relief oozed uncertainly from her mouth.

"Mister Smith," Graham put in. Smith turned to him. "I thought the same thing," Mike explained, "about Sabrina and C.W. After you said close contacts could be unwise. I've been following her like a shadow ever since, just watching. She's clean. Tough luck, but she is."

Smith turned away from Sabrina, and paced the floor again. "Maybe . . . maybe . . ." he muttered. Then he spun on his heel and brought the riding whip cracking down on

a glass table top. Leah jumped; Sabrina started involun-
tarily. Even Graham blinked.

"Find them!" Smith shouted. "We've got to find them!"

Poupon turned in triumph to Philpott. "Alors," he pointed
to the phone, "it was too easy, mon ami. They'll make the
first payment in five minutes from now. They're calling
Smith this very moment."

Philpott poked his head out of the van. "Did you hear
that, Sonya?" he asked.

"Got it," she said.

"Send it off to C.W.," Phlipott ordered. "And tell him
to welcome Graham to the organization."

"Check," Sonya replied. She worked the telegraph key,
and the reflector sent out a series of winking flashes.

Poupon sat back in his chair, and lit up a foul-smelling
pipe which had been banned from the conference room;
Philpott, though, was more tolerant. "One feels," Poupon
puffed, matches flying like kindling chips, "one feels we are
entering the final phase. Yet we have no idea in the world
how Smith can possibly get off that tower without us
locating him."

Philpott nodded moodily. He crossed the van to a table
in the corner, where the City Engineer's superintendent
was still pouring over his maps of dark and submerged
places known only to a few specialist moles with circles
under their eyes, whose company decent citizens normally
shunned.

"Are you absolutely certain," Philpott asked for at least
the tenth time, "that there aren't any underground connections—passages, that sort of thing—from the tower to
the subways, the metro, the sewers . . . anywhere?"

"I have told you, sir," the superintendent answered, con-
taining his patience masterfully, "there are none—at least,
none that are marked on the maps.

"The bases of the tower's four feet are self-contained.
You see—here, there, there, and here. Yes, there is an
electrical inspection chamber. We know they got into that,
apart from that, there are no tunnels, open sewers, metro
connections, no catacombs, priest-holes, potholes, lost
Egyptian tombs . . . beneath the tower there is nothing but

what should be there: power lines, water mains, pneumatics, and hydraulics. All of them, naturellement, are 'live '."

"Maintenance crawlways, then," Philpott persisted, hopefully.

The superintendent shook his delicately greying head. "Non, monsieur. Rien."

Philpott sighed his exasperation. Poupon suggested, "We know they have a helicopter, but of course they can't use it. The Air Force would blast it out of the skies."

"They would," Philpott agreed. "Once the lasers were off, anything that came near the tower would be scrap within minutes." He gnawed his lip, and said to Sonya, "I believe we're still missing something obvious. Read me back C.W.'s first message, would you, please?" he directed. "The bit about the techniques they practiced in training. I'm sure there was something there I overlooked."

Sonya started the transcription—but Philpott interrupted her with an urgent snap of his fingers. "Poupon!" he exclaimed. "Maybe you have it. The helicopter! If the helicopter is to be involved at all, the pilot will know precisely where and when he's supposed to pick up Smith."

He grew more excited. "Look—it's about time we broke up Smith's cosy little nest in the Loire Valley. Get the police in there—the Army, too. Don't smash up the place —not that you'd be allowed to. But find me that pilot, Poupon, and wring him dry. I want him singing like a bird by midnight."

Poupon inclined his head. "Consider it done, Monsieur."

Pei was on telephone duty in the restaurant again, and picked up the receiver when the bell chimed. He answered the call, and listened in silence. "A moment, please," he requested, "I shall contact Mister Smith."

He cradled the phone lengthways, and ran to the gallery. Smith was approaching with a search party, empty-handed. "The first payment, sir," Pei chattered, "it's ready; it's on the way. Fifteen million dollars. They've called—they're still on now—to confirm our readiness to receive it."

"Ahhhh," Smith beamed. "Max," he ordered a senior crewman, "train a searchlight on the front entrance. Pick up whoever's approaching the perimeter. Make sure there are no tricks. Then send two men down to get the money. Gentlemen, the bastards are crumbling. With any luck, we may be able to forget about Mrs. Wheeler."

Where the Pont d'Iéna bisects the Quai Branly on the river side of the tower, a heavily armored military truck pulled into the area of No-man's-land. Headlights blazing, the truck crossed to the Quai Branly perimeter, and a section of the barricade peeled away. Eight French soldiers got out of the back to join their young officer, who had traveled in the passenger seat.

Where the barricade had lain, one of the soldiers sketched a precise line in luminous paint. The officer chirped an order. The soldiers returned to the truck, and hauled out four aluminum suitcases. The lieutenant directed that they be placed in a group three feet short of the glowing boundary.

The powerful searchlight from the tower illuminated the pantomime, and also picked up two dark, hooded figures leaving the sanctuary of the tower base. They walked beneath the four great arches of its legs towards the perimeter. Each of the eight soldiers stood tensed and ready, weapons raised, fingers on trigger-guards. They were the tough men, the hard ones, the élite of the French Army; ruthless, daredevil fighters who had taken on the best in the world, and (sometimes) won.

Two men from the tower, their metal tags winking in the headlamp beam, stopped short. One whispered into a communicator. Smith, on the tower, brought his binoculars to a sharper focus, and rapped an order into his walkie-talkie.

One of the two detached himself and advanced to within a couple of feet of the painted line. He pointed at the suitcases and said, "Mister Smith wants them touching the line."

"Whereas my orders," the young officer replied, "are that they should stay where they are. If you want them, you will have to come and get them."

The commando blinked behind his mask, and measured the distance from the line to the cases. With eight trigger-happy soldiers there, whoever crossed the line to retrieve the cases was dead. He retreated to join his companion, and once more made contact with Smith.

Then both men came to within spitting distance of the line, and the commando spokesman said, firmly, "Put them on the line. If you do not, Mister Smith says he will not be responsible for the consequences."

The lieutenant shook his head. "I do not," he said, "take my orders from Mister Smith. Mine come from General Jaubert. Those are the orders I obey."

"On the contrary," spoke a new voice from behind the Saracen truck, "you will do as Mister Smith says." Philpott walked out and stood squarely facing the young lieutenant, in the glare of the lights. "Put the suitcases on the line," he directed.

"I do not know you, Monsieur," the officer replied.

"My name is Malcolm Philpott, and I have with me the Red priority directive of President Giscard D'Estaing." He thrust the affidavit before the lieutenant's eyes. "I am in charge of this operation, Lieutenant," Philpott went on, calmly.

"I have told General Jaubert once today already, that when I wish him to take an initiative, I will give him leave to do so. He has disobeyed my orders, and he will be held to account for it. Now"—his voice grew shaper—"put the suitcases on the line."

The lieutenant shuffled uncomfortably, and said, "One moment. I will check." He rounded the truck to the driver's seat, and picked up a walkie-talkie. Two minutes later he was back. "It will be as you say, Monsieur," he muttered. He gestured towards the cases, and two burly soldiers moved them carefully up to the phosphorescent marker, with their bases touching the gleaming paint.

Philpott barked, "You two—get what you came for." The commandos grinned, picked up a suitcase in each hand, and walked back to the tower.

They reported to Smith in the restaurant, where a team had been assembled to make a rough count of the fifteen million dollars. Smith listened in silence, and when the commando had finished, he rubbed his chin thoughtfully. "Describe Philpott," he ordered, "describe him minutely."

Both men obliged, and Smith ordered Leah to contact the château and run Malcolm Philpott through the master computer. It took the computer less than five minutes to deliver details of a man and an organization of which Smith had known next to nothing.

"UNACO?" he mused, incredulously. "Not the CIA, nor INTERPOL, nor the FBI? Not the US Army, or NATO? UNACO? Malcolm Philpott can afford to pay C.W. more than I can? I am opposed by a toothless professor, a bunch of civil servants and a few crank scientists? And I was getting worried?"

Smith laughed an ugly, barking laugh. He caught Leah by the arms and drew her to him. "Now I can afford to relax," he whispered. "I have been too long without your body. We will celebrate."

She smiled up at him. "Then let us drink first," she suggested.

"Spendid," Smith agreed. He called for champagne, and he and Leah, joined by Sabrina and Mike Graham, drank a toast, jubilantly proposed by Smith.

"To the United Nations Anti-Crime Organization—and Malcolm Gregory Philpott."

Graham looked across at Sabrina, and treated her to a long, slow wink.

C.W. crouched on the windowsill of the VIP room. The sole illumination still came from the chink of light peeping through the shield around the bulb. The black agent reached out, grabbed the nylon rope, hauled its trailing end up, and pulled it into the room.

C.W. looped the strong thread around him in mountaineer style, and played out the spare line. He turned to Adela Wheeler and said, "We're stuck in here, and it gives me bad vibes. I want out."

"I do, too," she replied, gamely.

"OK," C.W. nodded. "So how do you feel about heights?"

"They terrify me," she admitted.

C.W. nodded again. "That figures," he grunted. "Then close your eyes."

The count in the restaurant was going well. Two of Smith's commandos were trained in the so-called "banker's flip," and their moistened fingers flew at extraordinary speed through the neatly wrapped bundles of tens, hundreds, and thousands. Smith had left the menial work to his staff. He and Leah were now languorously joined, on a mattress in a room right next door to the VIP room.

Graham and Sabrina stood on the fringe of the counting group, hunched over a table in the center of the café. Occasionally, Sabrina let her attention wander. She never appreciated seeing other people's money, unless she had stolen it.

A vague flash of movement outside the restaurant window crept into the corner of her eye. She looked—and hissed a warning to Graham.

Clearly visible through the patchwork of girders, they saw C.W. sliding down the rope. Riding him piggyback, clutching his neck for dear life, her eyes tightly shut, was Adela Wheeler, in dark bloodstained combat fatigues.

They disappeared from view, and the tautened rope slipped back into its box-girder shell.

C.W. eased the rope out through clawed hands. Sweat ran down his face, and the wind blew Adela's thick lustrous grey hair across his eyes. He stopped his descent, balanced on a cross-strut, and moved so that she could stand alongside him, with his arm about her waist. C.W. cleared his brow on his sleeve. Adela was breathing heavily. "How much further?" she gasped, and made to look down at the ground.

C.W. caught her by the chin. "Don't even think of it," he commanded, fiercely. "Just remember, you're safe with me. I'm the best there is." She nodded mutely. C.W. helped her on to his back again, and muttered, "Not far to go, love. Not far now."

He swung out and inched down the face of the tower, his hands paying out rope, his bare feet caressing the struts. He drew in close again as he thought he heard movement from above. He looked up. Mike Graham and Sabrina crouched by the gallery railing, waved and urged him on.

C.W. smiled, and started the downward haul. And a protruding rivet caught a button of his combat safari jacket.

There was a soft ripping sound. C.W. froze, and looked about him. He dropped a few inches lower—and the ripping noise intensified. This time C.W. felt the tug on his clothing. He tried feeling his way back up but the snagged cloth would not release him.

The rivet now rested on the part of his jacket where the metal safety tag was pinned. Sabrina, on the gallery, gasped in horror, and Graham muttered a meaningless prayer.

C.W. said, "Hold tight, Adela. We're caught up on something." She got his neck in a vicious lock, and he allowed them to fall another foot down the rope.

With a final, ugly tearing sound that invaded the black man's brain like a death kneel. C.W.'s safety tag pulled free in its square of cloth.

It glided away into the darkness, lost amongst the tangle of ironwork.

C.W. was now defenseless against the laser guns, though Adela still wore Claude's metal tag on her breast.

CHAPTER
ELEVEN

Commissioner Poupon put the telephone down, and leaned back in his fragile, canvas-framed chair with an expression of beatific contentment across his pugnacious face. "So, my friend," he murmured to Philpott, "at last, action."

There was no reply. Poupon glanced over at his colleague: Philpott had slumped into a corner of the van, his head sunk on his chest. Poupon regarded him gravely, then rose, crossed the floor, and gently shook the sleeping man's shoulder.

Philpott jerked awake, looked up into Poupon's face, and rubbed his eyes. "Christ," he murmured, "that's a fine time for a catnap." He yawned, shook his head to clear the cobwebs, and asked the Commissioner if there had been any news.

Poupon indicated that there had. "We parachuted a hundred soldiers into the château," he said proudly. "It was all over in less than half an hour. The Château Clérignault still stands, as glorious as ever, but now it's in our hands."

Philpott climbed groggily to his feet. "Fantastic," he grinned. "And the chopper pilot? Did you get him?"

Poupon nodded. "Well?" Philpott demanded.

"His instructions," Poupon answered carefully, "are to pick up Smith at a particular point—on the River Seine."

"On the river?" Philpott exploded. "Where, for God's sake?"

148

"Well down from the Tour Eiffel," Poupon explained. "Between the Statue de la Liberté and the church of Notre Dame D'Auteuil—a kilometer and a half, perhaps."

Philpott jammed a fist petulantly into the palm of his hand. "Then how's he getting there?" he wondered. "It's a fair step from the tower to the river—all of it across open ground, most of it outside the laser perimeter. Even if he leaves the lasers on, he's vulnerable as soon as he's out of their range. It doesn't make sense, Poupon. It's crazy . . . no tunnels, no passages, no sewers. Is he going to burrow like a gopher?"

Poupon shrugged. "Je ne sais pas, Monsieur . . . we shall wait and see. But we have more urgent matters to consider, n'est-çe pas? Mrs. Wheeler, for example. Not to mention your agent—if he's still alive."

Philpott grimaced wearily. "Yeah," he admitted. "No word from C.W. for half an hour, at least. What the hell's happening up there?" Philpott punched the van wall, and rubbed his knuckles in frustrated rage.

C.W.'s rope ran out while he was still forty-odd feet from the ground. He shifted the burden of the woman on his back, adjusted her hold on his neck to a less suffocating angle, and muttered, "Hold on real tight now, baby. From here, it's the hard way. I may have to fly a little. But remember—you're safe. It'll be just like taking a bumpy elevator ride."

Adela Wheeler gave a scarcely audible squeaking reply, and C.W. committed their souls to providence and the formidable strength of his arms and legs.

Up aloft, the mouse-ear detectors sniffed the air and sought out the strange, moving mass descending the tower like a hunch-backed tarantula.

C.W. blinked the sweat out of his eyes, sniffed, and measured a cross-strut until he found a diagonal. He curled his toes around it, bent his body into a bow, and slid down to the next horizontal. Then he repeated the process.

Another Lap-Laser joined the gun monitoring their progress. It, too, twitched and stirred. Inside the computer, lying unwatched in the restaurant command post, a helix of silicon chips and wheels tried to sort out what was happening.

C.W. was tiring fast. His arms were straining from their sockets. His heart pumped blood around his body with a thud that he felt must penetrate even to Smith's lair. He knew he must rest . . . yet he could not be separated from Adela Wheeler. To do so was certain death—for both of them.

Unprotected, the lasers would seek him out for sure. And Adela Wheeler had no earthly hope of getting down by herself. She would stay rooted to the ironwork until fatigue claimed her body. And she would be grateful for the last despairing plunge into oblivion.

He gritted his teeth and swore fiercely, repeating one four-letter word over and over again. Mrs. Wheeler moaned through her pain. "I trust it's not me you want, Mr. Whitlock. And if it is, I only pray to God that you can wait for a more suitable time and place."

It was too much for C.W. He guffawed, and swung her off to stand by him, being careful to hold her close. He planted a big, smacking kiss on her lips. "You know, Mrs. W.," he said, "you're some doll. And a widow, too. And rich! I could do a great deal worse."

Adela smiled, and kissed him back on the cheek. "You're a naughty boy, C.W.," she murmured, "and I'd have been proud, proud and privileged, to have had you as a son, as well as Warren. You're my kind of man, and if you don't watch out, I'll ignore the forty years between our ages and show you a thing or two."

C.W. rolled his eyes, and did a passable imitation of a rampant stallion. Adela giggled, and C.W. said, "OK now. Back up. Hold on real well. The last bit's going to be a picnic."

At the first-level gallery rail, Mike grinned his relief. He had sent Sabrina back into the restaurant to cluster with the gloaters. Now he made to rejoin them himself. He ran into Smith and Leah, still flushed from their lovemaking.

"Taking the air, Mike?" Smith inquired.

"Money bores me, Mister Smith," Graham replied. "It's only spending it that I like."

"Then you'll enjoy the—uh—aftermath of this splendid little caper," Smith promised. Mike thought he heard the grunt of C.W.'s exertions below, and coughed to cover the tiny sound.

"Shall we go in with the others?" he suggested. Smith stood by and ushered first Leah, and then Graham, into the brightly lit café. He stayed for a second on the gallery, head cocked to one side, trying to make sense of the melange of buffeting wind and noises of the city and the night. Then he, too, walked into the restaurant. . . .

Although his rest, and the exchange with Mrs. Wheeler, had recharged his batteries, C.W. knew with total certainty that he could not face a prolonged, slow descent of the tower.

He gambled everything on his enormous strength. Grasping a horizontal, he bowed his body again and searched for the next cross-beam, perhaps eight feet away.

"Fasten your seat belt," he shouted to Adela above the wind. The pressure on his throat and chest increased. He gritted his teeth, and launched himself into thin air down the concave curve of the tower. His grasping hands clutched the cold beam, and he let out a shriek as the tremendous inertia cruelly racked his biceps and shoulder muscles.

"Are you going to do that again, C.W.?" Adela whispered.

"Uh-huh," he said. "And again, and again—and again." As the last word left his mouth he threw himself out once more, and dropped like a stone to the next horizontal strut.

Two to go . . . He half shimmied, half-slid down one, and triumphantly dropped the last few feet to the pavement, with Mrs. Wheeler still desperately leeched to his back. C.W. took most of the impact, but the President's mother came in for her share, and she almost shouted as the breath was forced from her lungs.

C.W. said, "Whatever else you do, don't let go of me. We're on the ground, and the difficult part could begin right now."

"Are we really there?" she asked, plaintively. "Did we climb down all that way—you with me on your back?"

"We sure did, ma'am," C.W. grinned. "We sure did—though when we tell people about it, they'll never believe us." C.W. felt like singing, but wisely resisted the impulse. Adela Wheeler kept a tight hold on him, and he turned in her arms to face her.

She saw the unimaginable strain in his face and said, "Did I hurt you?" solicitously.

"Strangled would be nearer the mark," C.W. winced. "Now, though, we have a problem."

He explained that he had lost his safety tag, and although the laser guns had not interefered with them when they were glued to the tower, it could be vastly different for the trip in open territory from the base to the perimeter.

"We've got just one tag between us," he said. "The one you're wearing—that Mike took from Claude. Now I don't know whether one safety strip held between two people is going to work or not. But we've got to try it. Having come this far, it'd be silly to stay here and get caught like rats in a trap whenever Smith decided to send somebody below. What do you say?"

Adela composed herself. "As I said on the dreadful man's television broadcast—and incidentally that was quite the worst I've ever made—I'm too ancient to start worrying about death now. If those—those things up there are going to kill us . . . then let them. I'll be dying with a man I admire—and that means a lot to a silly old woman like me. And in a good cause: the destruction of Smith. So— let's go, shall we?"

They started out, arms linked around each other, the safety tag held up by C.W. between their heads, his dark, tight curls resting on her soft but now straggling hair.

As they left the safety of the tower's bulk, C.W. glanced up, and could have sworn he saw the Lap Laser start to quiver.

Pei, back at the computer keyboard, shouted to Smith, "The lasers are tracking something! It's on the ground. It's got to be human. Moving erratically, but going away from the tower. A big blob!"

Smith rushed to the console, and cased the flickering screen. Then he shouted "Searchlight!" and ran out to the gallery rail.

Adela Wheeler and C.W. walked slowly but purposefully, measuring each other's paces, keeping their feet carefully aligned. C.W. felt his neck-hairs rise in the sights of the Lap Lasers.

And although he did not look around, he was right. Both laser guns had locked on to the shuffling pair. Both were now sending messages to the computer: does one tag cover two human beings?

Suddenly the man and woman were bathed in light from above. They could hear Smith snarl, "It's the black. He's got Mrs. Wheeler. Damn him. Oh, damn him."

Light came from the perimeter, too. Philpott danced in ecstasy. "You can make it, C.W., you can make it, sweetheart. Just a few more steps, you lovely guy. Just a few more."

C.W. grinned and shouted, "Would you shut the hell up. It's awkward enough without you capering around like a lunatic."

On the gallery, Smith bellowed, "Why aren't the guns firing. Goddammit?" Pei replied, "They've got a tag, sir. Whitlock's holding it above them. Claude's, I guess."

Tote uttered a roar of fury, and snatched a Kalashnikov from the man nearest him. He brought it to his shoulder and, before Smith could stop him, let off a stream of bullets at the sluggishly moving pair.

The tracer rounds followed the direct path on to which the Lap Lasers had already locked, and gleefully the guns recognized a viable target. Both barrels glowed, and the light beams cut the bullets from the air like fireflies snuffed out by marauding wasps.

Smith said, savagely, "That only makes us look foolish. We've lost them. Save your energy, and your ammunition. Cut the lights and come back inside, everyone. We still have work to do—and it's getting late."

Graham and Sabrina, standing next to Leah at the railing, exchanged glances. Graham found Sabrina's hand and squeezed it. She looked steadily at him and, not for the first time, liked very much what she saw. "First round to us," Mike whispered. She sniffed, cautiously. It was an eloquent reply.

As children would in a three-legged race, the President's mother and the Black Spiderman alternated their steps, and crossed the still-shining line of the perimeter, to be engulfed in a wildly excited throng. Adela Wheeler chose, however, to stay with her arms around C.W.'s neck, hugging him closely, sobbing at last, deeply and pathetically.

Then she released him, blinked back her tears, and surrendered to Philpott's welcoming embrace, while Sonya cuddled C.W. and told him how marvelous he was.

"Malcolm," said Adela, "I am grateful to you for arranging my release, and I am more than grateful to this wonderful boy here for carrying me down that tower, even though he treats me like a sack of potatoes."

Philpott chuckled, and said, "As long as you're safe, Adela—that's all that matters."

"But it's not," she insisted. "I meant what I said on television. I wouldn't have cared what happened to me. The important thing is to stop that atrocious man Smith. He's not human, Malcolm. He deserves to die."

"He'll be stopped, Adela," Philpott assured her. "Is there anything we can do for you now?"

"A bath," she considered, "something to eat, a stiff drink . . . that's enough for now. But first, I want to talk to Warren."

"He's holding on for you now," Philpott replied. "He's over the moon." And he led her to the communications van, where she picked up the telephone receiver and talked in gentle, stumbling tones to the President of the United States.

Philpott had installed a large color television set in the corner of the command van, and the unending banality of the fare, even with the sound turned down, was weighing on his nerves. But it had to be kept on; with his hostage plans thwarted, Smith, they felt, would need to reestablish his superiority in his customarily dramatic way.

There was a rap at the van door, and General Jaubert stumped in without waiting for an invitation. Ducret stood behind him, with a shrug for greeting. "Now, Monsieur Philpott, may I attack the tower?" the General demanded peremptorily.

Philpott looked up from the river plan he had been studying. "Ah, nice to see you, General," he observed. "I am pleased that you managed to curb the—ahem—laudable impetuosity of your renowned soldiers earlier this evening. If they had been permitted to proceed with their lunatic murder of Smith's commandos, I have no doubt whatsoever that Mrs. Wheeler would not be safe and well among us now.

"In answer to your question—no," Philpott went on firmly, "you may not attack the tower. I still believe that we can bring this operation to a successful conclusion without damaging either the Eiffel Tower or too many of the people in it. So please—withdraw to base. War, as somebody awfully clever once said, is too serious a business to be left to generals. We are at war with Smith. Should another delivery of money be planned, I shall be grateful if you do not interfere with it."

"But then, Monsieur," Jaubert put in cuttingly, "it is not your money, is it?"

Philpott considered the proposition. "That," he conceded, "is a fair point. However, if we are to save any of it, I must insist we do it my way—and President Giscard D'Estaing agrees with me."

"Another politician," Jaubert snorted. Philpott was about to frame a barbed response when Poupon raised his hand for silence, and jumped to the TV set. As he turned up the sound, Smith's face appeared, replacing a young girl singer with a deeply cleft bosom and frizzy green hair, whom the Commissioner secretly admired. Smith was as relaxed and urbane as ever.

"Good evening, ladies and gentleman of France," he began. "Once more, I have to apologize to you for breaking so rudely into your evening's enjoyment of television, but I have some news for you. I also wish to address a few remarks to Interior Minister Ducret—and to the United Nations Anti-Crime Organization and its commander, Malcolm Philpott."

There was only one place, Smith knew, where that bombshell would explode—and he was right. The atmosphere inside the command post was electric. Philpott faltered and turned appealingly to Poupon—then the frown left his face. His gaze, bitter and resentful, switched to Jaubert. "Of course," he gritted. "I had to unmask myself in dealing with your bloody soldiers. Obviously Smith's man took the word back to him. Now the whole world knows about us."

"Do not worry, mon ami," cautioned Poupon softly. "People forget these things. They've probably forgotten already." Jaubert, for once, was suitably cowed.

Smith went on, "I wish to thank Minister Ducret, Finance Minister LeGrain, and indeed the entire French Government, for the fifteen million US dollars you have so kindly donated to my worthy cause. Many of you watching me may not yet be aware that my hostage, Mrs. Adela Wheeler, has elected to leave the tower. I had always intended that she should go from here unharmed, but I would have chosen a safer and less painful mode of exit for her.

"And incidentally, Mr. Philpott, I'm glad your agent, Whitlock, got back to you. Your other people here may not be so lucky."

It was a pure guess—inspired intuition from a master of deception. Philpott leapt to his feet, swearing. Poupon rose swiftly and caught his arm. "He's probably bluffing, Monsieur," the Commissioner urged. "I can see you're not a poker player."

Philpott breathed deeply and nodded. "You're right," he said, "he could be. And you're right about me; I don't play poker. University professors seldom do."

"Then relax," Poupon advised. "Smith hasn't finished with us yet."

Smith had a condescending sneer on his face. "Don't take it too hard, Philpott," he continued. "You have never crossed swords with someone of my caliber before. Maybe this will teach you a salutary lesson."

Philpott mumbled, "Christ, if he's not bluffing, then I've sacrificed two very fine people."

Ducret shook his head. "No, Malcolm," he said, "they've sacrificed themselves. As you yourself put it, this is war. Your people are soldiers. They are expected to know the odds, and to take the risks. I am sorry, but soldiers are expendable. It was ever so, and it always will be."

Philpott grinned, wryly. "Perhaps I'm in the wrong job," he said.

"I don't think so," Ducret rejoined, "I really don't think so."

Their attention returned to the television set. Smith was saying, "This—uh—turn of events has, however, forced a change in my plans. As I said, I have received half of my thirty-million-dollar ransom. Well, I am not a vindictive man, nor a particularly greedy one, despite what the lately departed Mrs. Wheeler said about me earlier.

"The fact is, the French authorities are growing increasingly devious. Given a few more hours," he smiled patronizingly, "and heaven know's what mischief they'd get up to. In effect, I do not choose to wait around and find out.

"I and my followers will leave the Eiffel Tower in"—he glanced at his watch—"in about fifteen minutes. I have observed that there are television outside-broadcast units here. I have little doubt that they will take out the scheduled program, and keep you tuned to our escape. It will, I assure you, be worth the effort. It will also, from my point of view, be entirely successful.

"So, for the last time, I bid you good night, and thank you for your immensely kind cooperation. I shall miss my beautiful Loire château—which I bequeath to the nation. Au revoir, més amis." And he was gone.

Jaubert groaned theatrically, and Philpott muttered, "Fifteen minutes. It's not long." To Sonya he said, "Get C.W. Let's think this thing through properly."

Smith rose from the chair before the television camera, and said to the French crew. "Your usefulness is at an end. Thank you for what you have done." The cameraman looked pale; his soundman hid his face in his hands. Smith smiled crookedly, and motioned to Leah. "It is time," he said. "I slipped a coded message into the TV script to bring the helicopter in ahead of time. So now—I must go."

"Be careful, then," she warned.

"Am I not always careful?" Smith quizzed her. She nodded her head slowly. "Of course. Shall I see you below?"

"You go ahead," Smith ordered, "I will join you down there. Use the stairs; they're lit now."

With a thoughtful, even regretful, expression on his face, he watched her body sway down the iron steps. . . .

C.W. elbowed his way past a group of soldiers and climbed into the communications van. "Mrs. W.'s OK," he announced. "She's resting. Say, she's really something."

"So are you, according to her," Philpott grinned. "But we've got more important things to attend to." He filled the black agent in on the latest developments arising from Smith's telecast. C.W. whistled. "Jeeze, that barely leaves us time to come up with something."

"Think, then, C.W.," Philpott urged. "We know he's

being lifted up from the river by the helicopter: but how in God's name is he getting to the river? Think, man, think."

C.W. protested, "I am, for Christ's sake, I am." He pulled a face, scratched his woolly head, and spat out a shred of tobacco.

"He can't just disappear," Philpott persisted. "There has to be a clue, somewhere. Something we've all overlooked. Now what is it, C.W.? Huh?"

C.W. swore and ran his hands over his aching head. "He's—he's been a step ahead of us all the time," he ventured hesitantly. "We haven't really known what he's been up to at all." He looked at Philpott, Sonya, and Poupon anxiously. "There was only one thing that I found out which I honestly felt I wasn't meant to learn. I don't know, though. It may mean nothing—you know, it could be a wild goose chase, and while we're on it, Smith could be getting clean away by some other means."

"What is it?" Philpott demanded. "Tell us, C.W. It doesn't matter if you're wrong, because it's the only thing we've got to go on."

"W-e-l-l," the agent began, with infuriating slowness, "it's this: I stumbled into something curious in the basement inspection chamber. You know, the power lines are there. We were lacing cable into the mains' supply; it was thirsty work, and I wanted a beer." He stopped. They waited. "Well?" Philpott spluttered.

"I spotted a couple of beer tanks—cylinders with taps. They came in with the caterers. They were standing in the corner of the inspection chamber. I went to one and stuck my head under it. I turned the spigot—but nothing came out. Just—air."

"Air?"

C.W. nodded. "Compressed air. Oxygen."

Philpott's mouth opened and closed. He gnawed a finger-nail; Poupon looked totally perplexed. Then Philpott snapped his fingers, and a look of sheer delight possessed his face.

"Oxygen cylinders!" he roared. "That's it! By George, C.W., that's it." He rushed to the table and yanked the distinguished-looking City Engineer's superintendent out of his chair. Philpott thumbed through the maps, plans, and sketches, and found the tower base section.

"There!" he speared the latticework of cables and pipes. "See? Water mains. He's going to get out through a water main! That's why he wants oxygen cylinders. The mains have got inspection and repair hatches, haven't they?" he barked at the engineer.

"They have," the superintendent agreed. "There is one right here." He traced with the tip of his pencil a dotted-line section of the pipe passing through the Eiffel Tower's basement chamber.

"Where can he come out?"

"Anywhere he pleases, if he's got the right equipment," the superintendent said, fetching over a sewage and water system plan.

"In the Seine?" Poupon cut in.

The superintendent spread his hands eloquently. "Of course. The pipes empty straight into the river—the big main pipes, that is. It is much easier for a diver to examine them there than to dig up a length of road or install an inspection hatch under a manhole."

Philpott scratched his head, and his eyes lit up once more. "Is there an outlet," he asked, eager but reluctant to hear the answer, "anywhere near the bateaux mouches out there on the river?"

The superintendent again consulted the plan. "Indeed there is," he announced. They drew back, and looked questioningly at each other.

"Worth the risk?" Philpott put to Poupon and C.W.

Poupon replied, "It's your decision, Monsieur."

Philpott duly debated it with himself for a full minute. "Then it's worth it," he announced. "This is what we do. . . ."

As he started to outline the plan forming in his mind, a great shout went up from the crowd outside, lining the perimeter now in ever-growing numbers since the outside TV broadcasts began. Sonya pushed her way to the door of the van, and gasped.

C.W. stood at her elbow, and gazed in astonishment at the tower. He whistled admiringly and muttered, "Will you look at that now? The crazy bastard's started a fireworks display. Real fireworks."

Poupon chuckled. "Smith must be French," he reflected. "He may be mad—but he has a truly Gallic sense of style."

Expert pyrotechnicians in Smith's crew had arranged the display in the little top gallery. It was one of the most dazzling ever seen in Paris—like Bastille Day, the Fifth of November, and the Fourth of July all rolled into one.

Stunning rainbow bursts erupted from the tower to bathe the night sky in vivid washes of spectral colors. Stars rained over the enthralled crowds, and mighty explosions sent jet-streams of gold and silver, green and blue, and garish orange soaring up to fizz and crackle, to subdivide, and eventually to die in cascades of glowing embers.

The watching people actually cheered themselves hoarse at the finale. Thin, strong poles projecting invisibly from the foot of the television mast supported a scale model, picked out in tiny Catherine wheels and modest little color showers, of—the Eiffel Tower. For accompaniment, Roman candles sent charges of silver diamonds and golden sunbursts climbing ever higher into the wind, and the tower's public address system played the Marseillaise.

Poupon stood at attention until Philpott jogged his arm and said, "It's probably only a cover for something spectacularly nasty."

On the first landing, Smith looked out over the rolling parkland at the sea of upturned faces. "Adieu," he whispered, "you have given me a fitting salute to my victory. I shall remember you . . . and you will remember me."

The commandos and remaining hostages poured into the elevator on Smith's instructions. He took a key from his pocket and handed it to Pei.

The Asian inserted it into a keyhole in a red box bearing a DANGER! stamp. Next to the key sat an innocent-looking black button. Smith nodded briskly and said, "Arm it."

Pei pressed the button. "The—the—d-detonators are now fully armed, Mister Smith," he stammered. "We have ten minutes. And there is, I'm afraid, no way you can change your mind."

Smith replied, "I am not in the habit of changing my mind."

He glanced at the set of stout canvas bags leaning against

the railing. Pei stood over them, and looked up at Smith. "Shall I put them in the elevator?" he asked.

Smith grinned—a knowing, sinister smile. "No, Pei," he said, "I'll take charge of the money now. You get into the elevator with the others."

There was a mutter of alarm from the lift. Smith stalked to the rail and stood with his back to it. His machine-pistol was leveled at the crew. "Pei," he waved the gun at the Asian, "do as you were told."

Pei squeezed into the elevator next to Graham and Sabrina, and Smith rapped at the newly released elevator operator, "Close the gates."

The heavy iron gates crashed into position. "Gentlemen, and Miss Carver," Smith sneered, "you have all performed magnificently. However, from this point I no longer have any need for your services. I thank you warmly for what you have done for me, and I sincerely wish you were able to enjoy the successful conclusion as much as I shall.

"But that cannot be," he went on, as a paralyzing fear overcame the commandos in the elevator. "Since I am leaving with only half the ransom I claimed, you are—how shall I put it?—ah . . . an unwarrantable expense. I simply cannot afford the luxury of paying you. Goodbye—and God speed."

He chuckled, and shouted "Down!" at the petrified elevator operator. The man pressed the button as a reflex action, and the elevator sank complainingly out of sight.

Smith fingered the transmit button of his walkie-talkie and said to Leah, "Are you ready?" From the small red box came the steady, relentless tick of the metronome timer. Leah replied that she was. "Then proceed, please," Smith ordered.

Leah's hand hovered over a lever on the wall—the isolator to the main power supply to the tower, though not affecting the secondary generators which powered the lasers. She threw the switch, and Smith, peering into the lift shaft, watched with satisfaction as the elevator shuddered to a halt.

The ransom bags were linked at their necks by a leather thong, and Smith took a nickel protection tag from his pocket and clipped it to the strap. Then he stooped, hoisted up the bags, and heaved them over the side.

The two west-facing laser guns followed the same path as Smith's eyes in tracking the bags to the ground. The mouse-ears moved, but the guns obeyed the metal tag.

Smith moved further along the railing to a coil of rope already looped around it and fastened tightly. The rope led to one of the four massive arches between the legs of the tower. He shimmied down it and dropped to the ground. He smiled at the thought that his descent had been a great deal easier than C.W.'s . . . the black agent had had to drop through the structure of the tower, carrying a burden which, Smith admitted, most men would have found insupportable.

With the generators roaring defiantly at the massed troops and guns, and still in the circle of protection afforded by his trucks, Smith made for the electrical inspection chamber on the last lap of his escape from the hostage tower.

On the way, almost as an afterthought, he scooped up fifteen million dollars that someone had left lying around. . . .

Panic spread like a forest fire through the elevator. Graham clutched Pei's arm and gritted, "The charges? Are they armed?" Dumbly, Pei nodded. He sought Tote, and rested his head on the big man's shoulder.

Mike pounded the glass side of the elevator in rage and fear. "That bastard!" he shouted, "Oh that—bastard." Then his eye fell on the metal bench that formed the only seating in the elevator.

"Give me a hand," he shouted to Pei. The Indonesian leapt to the other end of the bench and grasped it. Together they lifted it up, and used it as a battering-ram to smash one of the windows of the elevator.

There was a mad scramble to get to the shattered window, but the opening was too small. "Again!" Mike screamed, "again!" They backed a few paces, and charged once more at the windows. Another went under the hammer-blows—and another; and a central strut.

It was enough, and Sabrina was brutally felled to the floor in the heedless stampede. Graham helped her to her feet, and said swiftly, "You realize what you have to do."

He jerked his head aloft. She said, "Yes . . . if there's time."

"There's *got* to be," Mike returned. "At least we have to try. You know that, Sabrina." She blinked and said, "OK, Mike. And you?"

"I'm going after Smith," he said grimly. She turned to scale the cab and the tower, and Graham called softly, "Sabrina." She looked back. "Good luck, sweetheart," he said. "And take care. Please?" She nodded. "And you, Mike." He thought she had never looked lovelier—or more terrified.

Graham perched on a cross-beam and saw Smith's escape rope swaying just out of reach in the wind. He clasped an upright and leaned out. His fingertips barely touched the hemp strands, and as they did the rope moved tantalizingly away again.

Mike breathed a heartfelt sigh and muttered, "C.W., C.W. where are you?"

Then he took a firm, balanced stance on the cross-beam, lowered his body into a crouch, cursed Malcolm Philpott quite vilely, and sprang into the night. His fingers clutched frantically for the rope—and found it. He shed some skin from his burning hands as he slithered at least eight feet, but then he caught the rope in a firmer grasp, and slid to the foot of the tower, searching in vain for any trace of the vanished Smith. . . .

Sabrina sighted her target—the nearest explosive charge —ten feet above her head.

She estimated she had probably six minutes in which to disarm not one, but four, bombs.

Dangling outside the ribs of the tower she spotted Smith's rope, which Graham had just abandoned. She calculated she could reach two charges on the rope, which would save her precious climbing time. She made for it, caught it more easily than Mike had done, and swarmed up the tower to the bomb that, on the west-facing side, was furthest away from her.

Sabrina planted her feet on a cross-strut, anchoring the rope between her legs. She studied the plastique charge, wedged into the hollow of the box girder. Deep inside the cloying, deadly putty was the live detonator. Cautiously, she reached out a hand, fingers trembling, her teeth trapping her full bottom lip.

A hurricane gust of wind rose up behind her and howled through the tower. She was literally blown into the girder, her face no more than six inches from the bomb, her questing fingers splayed out over the plastique, yet not touching the wired detonator. She clung there, knuckles white, eyes rounded in horror.

The timer in the little red box ticked round to 5:15, 5:14, 5:13. . . .

Graham combed the vault beneath the tower, but Smith had left no trace of his presence. "Where in hell's he gone?" Mike queried to himself.

The smallest of sounds came from behind him, and Graham whirled around, alarm on his face but savage power in the set of his body and the menace of his arms and hands. C.W. sauntered out past a generator truck and drawled, "Hi." He still wore Claude's safety tag.

Mike relaxed. "Smith?" he asked. "Any ideas?"

"Sho' has, boss," C.W. replied, then dropped his bantering tone. "He's in the inspection chamber in the basement. We figure he's getting out through a water main."

"A water main!" Mike groaned. "Christ alive, of course. That'd be the only thing that makes sense."

"Where's Sabrina?" C.W. put in.

Graham pointed upwards. "She's got her hands full," he said. "Five minutes or so to disarm four big fat bombs—or bingo, and up she goes."

"Shit," said C.W. "OK, I'm on my way."

He jumped for the rope, and made it to the first level almost as quickly as Mike had climbed down. . . .

Leah Fischer lifted a red "beer tank" and settled it on Mister Smith's back, alongside a bulky pack. The tank now had straps fixed to it, and tubes ran from the top. She turned a tap.

As C.W. had discovered, the tanks contained not beer, but oxygen. For Leah and Smith, they served as air tanks.

Smith winked at Leah behind his face mask. Like her, he had a breathing tube clamped between his teeth.

Smith had already removed a manhole-sized inspection plate from one of the huge conduits carrying water power beneath the streets of Paris. He peered into the hole. The pipe had a diameter of four feet, and foaming water raced through it under pressure.

He had hooked the loop of a nylon line over one of the rusting bolt-heads. The end of the line disappeared into the rushing torrent. . . .

Hundreds of feet above them, on the wind-battered Eiffel Tower, Sabrina Carver's slim fingers reached out once more to stop tentatively an inch short of the embedded detonator.

The timer ticked remorselessly on. 4:22. 4:21. 4:20.

CHAPTER
TWELVE

Smith motioned to Leah to turn off his oxygen tap. He pushed up the rubber mask, and let the breathing pipe drop from his mouth.

She looked at him, an unspoken query on her face. He gently lifted her mask off and teased the tube out from between her strong white teeth.

Leah had a sudden premonition, yet dared not give voice to it. But she knew Mister Smith . . . better than he imagined.

Smith's voice was like an evil caress, a touch from the grave: like the breath of Satan.

"Leah, you have alway pleased me greatly," he purred. "I could not have asked for a better companion. You have been loyal, inventive, daring; you share my glorious vision of crime as a redeeming force, a power that can cleanse the soul and uplift the spirit.

"But Leah . . . dear, faithful Leah; my brave passionate friend."

Leah's mouth was dry with the sour taste of fear. Smith saw burgeoning panic in her eyes, those blue-green eyes that regarded him normally with such undiscriminating adoration. He touched her face, stroked the rounded cheek; he let his finger trace the curve of her eyebrow, and smiled understandingly as she tried to speak but couldn't, the words lodged in her throat like uninvited guests.

"It's simply that . . . I'm tired of you, Leah." The fingers

166

wandered down the other cheek, trailing over her ear, and settling on her smooth neck.

"I need a change, my pet. Besides, you will be an encumbrance on the journey I am planning to take. You will slow me down, Leah. I cannot permit that to happen. You are, I regret to say, dispensable. Superfluous."

Leah found the words at last, and they came tumbling out: declarations of love, protestations of faith, words of pleading . . . begging.

Smith's manicured hand still rested on her neck. "Of course, of course, Leah, of course I understand. And we shall meet again, as you say. One day. Who knows? But for now, sweet Leah, this is"—he paused and chuckled as the thought occurred to him—"this is one bath I shall be taking alone."

He laughed, found the pressure point in her neck, dug his finger into it, and carefully caught her as she slumped unconscious to the concrete floor.

"We can't have you damaged now, can we?" he murmured. "I don't like pretty things to be hurt—and you are a pretty little thing, Leah." Her unseeing eyes looked up at him.

"Yet I believe," Smith went on, as though she could hear him, "that I actually heard you say one day that I was 'boring,' was it? Did you think I'd forgotten that, Leah? Oh no, my dear. Mister Smith never forgets anything."

He had cradled her head, and now he let it fall on to the stonework. Her mouth gaped open, and only the rise and fall of her breasts showed that she was still alive.

Smith readjusted his mask and tube, and set the air tank's tap once more to on. He shook his head sadly, and lowered himself into the water main. His hand holding the rim of the inspection hatch, he uncoupled the nylon thread from the bolt, and pulled on it.

Three blue rubberized diver's bags swam into view. They were linked together; fat, bulbous cylinders, like monstrous sausages.

Smith smiled and released them, keeping hold of the end of the line.

The king-sized hot dogs and the swiftly moving current pulled him to the Seine.

* * *

Sabrina's tremulous fingers touched the detonator. Holding her breath, she hooked her thumbnail and fingernail around the live wire.

Millimeter by millimeter, with sticky globules of plastique clinging to it, the detonator slid out. It freed itself from its vicious mooring with an obscene plop.

Sabrina groaned and murmured a long, drawn-out "H-e-e-e-y." She let the detonator fall from her hand, and it plummeted to earth.

"One down," she breathed. "Three to go. Ah well—"

The clock dial on the red box showed 3:52. 3:51. 3:50. 3:49. . . .

Graham launched himself furiously against the door of the inspection chamber. It splintered under his charge, and he brust into the room in a crouch, prepared to sell his unprotected life dearly.

He pulled up short, taking in the open water main, the unconscious woman—and the line of bubbles leading out to the river.

Without a second's hesitation he bent down, ripped the mask and tube from Leah's front and the tank from her back, donned them swiftly, and dropped into the fast-flowing stream. . . .

Sabrina squirmed down the flailing rope, and pulled up short, jamming her feet against the tower struts, opposite the next charge. Her head told her to get on with the job: to disarm the second, the third, the fourth bombs.

Her heart told her there just wasn't time. When the mighty tower buckled and plunged to the ground in a tangle of twisted iron, she would still be on it. She sniffed, and approached the muddy-grey mess of plastique.

Crew members and hostages jumped off the tower to freedom or arrest as C.W. clambered up the spidery frame and snapped on a torch to locate Sabrina. He spotted her with her hand easing into the heart of a girder, and he wisely kept silent.

Then he saw her holding a detonator, clinging to the swaying rope and wiping her streaming brow on the shoulder-piece of her combat jacket.

"Sabrina—it's me. How many have you got?"

She followed the beam of light to its source. "Oh, thank God you're here, C.W. We may have a chance now. Not a big one, but at least a chance. This is my second—" She tossed the detonator into the wind. "I've done the west and south pillars. I haven't touched east or north. Take whichever you like."

C.W. galvanized his weary body into action, and scrambled over the tower as if his life depended on it.

Which it did.

The timer clicked on. 2:48. 2:47. 2:46. 2:45. . . .

Arc-lamps were now trained on the tower from all sides. At the communications van, Ducret and Poupon followed through binoculars every agonizing second of the battle to save their preposterous tower.

"We don't know precisely when the charges were armed," Poupon replied, puffing his pipe into Ducret's face, "but there can't be more than three of Smith's fifteen minutes remaining. So—" he shrugged expansively.

"I hope to God Philpott knows what he's doing," Ducret commented. "Presumably there's been no sign of Smith among the men we captured?"

Poupon shook his grizzled head. "Nothing. But *I* think Philpott knows what he's doing, Monsieur le Ministre. And I hope to God that those two on the tower do, as well."

2:01. 2:00. 1:59. . . .

C.W. strained out over the spiral section of staircase and lunged for the playful rope. The wind gusted again, but this time it favored the good. The rope flew to his hand.

He grabbed it thankfully, and launched himself into space, swinging out in a wide arc, and surging back towards the east pillar at a dangerous speed. At the girder junction, C.W. took one hand off the rope and clawed for a cross-beam. His fingers connected, but the strut was slick with evening dew, and it slipped from his grasp.

C.W.'s body slammed into the pillar and bounced off. He shouted and swore, and kicked himself away to come in again at a less acute angle. With a sharp slap, his hand found the cross-beam, and locked on to it.

He trapped the precious rope and, as Sabrina had twice done, wedged it safe as he faced the east-pillar bomb.

His hand snaked out—but his naked foot, curled on the lower cross-strut, skidded off. He grunted and made a wild sweep for the girder, hooking his heel painfully on to the horizontal.

"Cool, baby, cool," he breathed. "Play it like diamonds —or that gorgeous Chinese horse."

Summoning all his nerve and skill, C.W. throttled down, and carefully drew out the detonator.

He looked around wildly, and saw Sabrina making her way as best she could towards the north flank.

The dial on the concealed timing device beeped under the minute mark.

"Leave it, honey!" he screamed, and set off across the tower like a demented acrobat. Again—as he had with Adela Wheeler on his back—C.W. chose the hard way. He abandoned climbing when he reached a point he thought was level with the charge, swung himself up to a horizontal I-beam, and ran across it at full tilt, unseeing and uncaring.

The timer marked off the vanishing seconds. 23. 22. 21 . . . . .

Sabrina had also lost all sense of fear. Reckless of the danger, she unknowingly raced C.W. from the opposite side of the tower, and they collided in a tangle of arms and legs at the north-pillar junction. The timer stood at nine seconds—and counting.

"Where the—is it?" C.W. gasped, feeling in the box of the girder.

"Oh my God," Sabrina cried, "we're too low. It's up there!" She pointed above their heads. The blob of plastic with its wired catalyst rested out of their reach.

Four seconds.

"Up!" C.W. screamed, making a cradle. Frantically, she hooked her foot into his clenched hands and he levered her into the air.

It was no time for finesse. No time for anything.

Two seconds.

She dipped her fingers into the plastic, drew out the detonator, and tossed it back over her head.

One second. Zero. Ignition!

The detonator exploded in mid-air. Simultaneously, the

three from the other pillars fired where they lay on the ground.

Sabrina Carver locked her ankles around the neck of C. W. Whitlock and her arms around the cold iron column and cried into the wind.

But the Eiffel Tower was safe.

The wide mouth of the water main opened on the bank of the Seine, and coughed up three plump sausages and a man in a black wetsuit.

Smith surfaced, peered through his mask in every direction, and kicked strongly for the rubberized ransom bags. He collected them, hauled his body onto the leading bag, and struck out downriver towards an anchored bateau mouche.

Two minutes later, a second black-suited, tanked figure shot from the pipe in the powerful current and was tossed head over heels into the river. Graham flapped like an ungainly, paddling dog, clawed his way to the surface, and tred water.

He, too, looked this way and that. Light flooded on to the Seine from behind him, and from the glow of street lamps. He saw his fast-crawling quarry on the buoyant raft, and noiselessly set out after him.

Smith reached the bateau mouche, grasped the ladder, and pulled himself up on deck. He had tied the nylon thread around his waist, and he reached down to tug the bags to the side of the boat and drag them in.

Mike abandoned his churning crawl, and settled into a quieter breaststroke. His passage through the even surface of the water created hardly a ripple.

Smith stowed the ransom bags away, and padded over to the helm of the bateau mouche. He started the engine. It came to life with a sudden roar.

Smith ran forward and cast off the bowline, leaving it trailing. He was doubling back the length of the boat to cast off the sternline, when he spotted the dark shape angling in towards the stern.

Smith had no gun with him. Nor was there one on the boat. Nonetheless, he was not completely unarmed. Smith was never completely unarmed.

But he chose not to tangle with the newcomer. Instead, he threw off the sternline, and felt the bateau mouche drift slowly away on the current. He sped forward again, to take his place at the helm. A smile played on his lips.

His hands closed on the gear-shift levers, and Smith threw both engines into reverse. Then he jammed the throttles up to full speed.

The river foamed and boiled under the plunging boat, and Smith, standing at the door of the wheelhouse, peered into the spume passing the bow.

His smile changed to a broad grin as a solitary air tank, its strap torn and hanging loose, floated by.

Smith turned and reentered the wheelhouse. He eased the throttles back, and levered the gearshift to forward.

The bateau moche chugged amiably down the Seine, different from the other boats taking the night air only in the respect that it sported minimal lights.

He whistled, and occasionally looked out through the window above the helm. He scanned the sky, fell silent, looked out again—and, once more, fell to whistling. It was a jaunty little sea shanty. English, Smith thought. Great seafaring race, the English.

Large rubber tires formed a waterline frieze along the side of the bateau mouche, and Mike Graham clung groggily to the last in line. He dragged himself up the side of the boat, and slithered over the rail to land in a wet heap on deck.

Mike lay there for a few moments getting his breath and his senses back. Then he climbed to his feet, and crept past the benches under their striped awning towards the bow. He sidled up to the wheelhouse, and peeped through the glass door.

He met Smith eyeball to eyeball.

Smith throttled back, and put his engine in neutral. He leaned down, as if he had all the time in the world, and casually drew a long-bladed knife from a sheath at his right leg.

Graham saw light winking on the metal, and backed away. Smith jerked open the door and moved in eerie silence out on to the slippery deck.

Warily, they circled, Smith's keen eyes ranging over

Graham from head to foot. He registered no surprise when he saw who it was. The fact that the Eiffel Tower had not blown didn't particularly distress him. He had his ransom, and the escape path was clear. Well, almost. And if anyone among his crew was to survive and elude capture, Smith would have bet on Mike Graham.

Smith was finally satisfied that Graham was not armed. He danced in like the practiced knife-fighter he was, arm held low, the knife sitting easily in his upturned hand, twisting and turning, perfectly balanced.

But Mike Graham, too, was a master of many forms of combat. He knew knife-fighters well, and had long since diagnosed their strengths and weaknesses. The weaknesses he had found many ways of exploiting: and the strengths he was adept at turning against the man with the dagger.

Although Smith kept his body and skills in shape, he rarely had to use them in earnest. Smith fought like he fenced—elegantly, correctly, as a gentleman should, obeying the rules.

Mike Graham was no gentleman. For him, the rule book didn't exist.

Graham started to close, looking over-confident. Smith took half a pace back, as if in fear—then whipped his lithe body forward and down, his knife arm shooting out, the blade as rigid as a natural extension of his hand, striking straight and true for Graham's heart.

But Mike's whole move had been a feint to trap Smith into a committed lunge. He leaned his torso to the right like a bullfighter, and lashed out his foot at Smith's leading leg.

The kick caught Smith right on target—just below the kneecap. He hardly had time to squeal with pain when the second heel kick landed in his groin. Two inches to the left and he would have been Miss Smith.

He was still in a half-crouch, and Graham closed again. Well-supported now on his left leg, he brought his right knee in and uppercut Smith on the point of his smoothly shaven chin.

The blow loosened four of Smith's bottom teeth, and shook his individual vertebrae to a point halfway down his back. His head swam, his eyes shot out of focus, and Graham jerked his unresisting knife-arm.

Mike caught the wrist in a cruel grip with his left hand, and locked his right arm around Smith's in a twisting judo hold. Smith winced and squealed again, and the knife left his unclenched fingers to clatter on the deck.

Graham beat him to the dagger, and turned on Smith with ugly triumph in his eyes. But Smith had scampered away. He headed for the wheelhouse, jumped on a barrel, and vaulted up to the roof of the bateau mouche.

Mike followed him by another route, and was facing him on the flat, scoured planks before Smith could take any preventive stance. They measured each other, shivering inside their wetsuits, panting and angry. Smith conceded that Graham was more than a match for him in a dirty fight; he also conceded that there was no way Mike was going to fight cleanly.

He judged that Graham could very easily use the knife on him, with little provocation. He decided to compromise by talking his way out of trouble. Smith had done that more than once; his natural bent for treachery made conversation, for him, almost as deadly a weapon as a knife or a sword.

His decision was influenced by a sound that was music to his ears: the hum of an approaching helicopter. It was low at first, though unmistakable. Now it rose in intensity.

"Well, Graham," Smith began, "so the day goes to you. Congratulations."

Mike ignored him.

"I imagine you also put my laser guns out of commission?"

Graham shook his head, and said "No."

Smith raised his eyebrows. "Whitlock?" he inquired.

Again, Mike replied, "No."

"Then who?"

Graham smiled. "Sabrina Carver. At least, I told her to."

Smith's face clouded. "She was in it, too," he mused. "A pity. I rather liked her. I was contemplating offering her a —mmm—position, in my organization. How fortunate that I resisted the temptation."

Graham nodded. Smith rubbed his aching jaw. The noise of the helicopter grew louder.

Smith said, "She and C.W. are with Philpott, I imagine."

"Indeed," Mike remarked.

Smith raised his voice and suggested a division of the spoils. "Is that what you have in mind, Mike?" he asked. "Surely it must be, now that you have the whip hand."

Graham shook his head, slowly but decisively.

"Money on this scale doesn't attract you?" Smith queried acidly.

Graham said, "It's not what I want, Smith."

"And what do you want? Me?"

Mike looked steadily at him. The helicopter seemed to be circling overhead now, but Graham was concentrating his whole attention on Smith.

"Libya," he shouted, "four years ago. Remember? You sold Russian weapons to a group of crazy terrorists. You *couldn't* forget that, Smith, could you?"

Smith inclined his head superciliously. "It strikes," he admitted, "a familiar note."

"A CIA agent was on to you," Mike persisted. "You boobytrapped his car. Do you remember that, Smith?"

The other man shrugged. "It's all in the game. Sometimes one has to order retaliatory actions which one finds personally distasteful."

"Distasteful!" Graham echoed. "Yes, it was. Because, you see, you didn't kill the CIA agent. You killed his wife. She was pregnant, with their only child."

The sneer left Smith's face. He swallowed, though it was difficult for him. "*Your* . . . wife?" he ventured.

Mike nodded. His hate-filled eyes were slits now, his muscles bunched, his teeth bared. "And since then, Smith," he snarled, "there hasn't been one second of any day or night that I haven't been on your trail."

He started forward, the knife held before him, glinting ominously, the instrument of his revenge.

"For you, Mister Smith," he hissed, "it's the end of the line."

Suddenly they were bathed in light from the helicopter, coming down out of the night sky like a stone. Mike looked up, and was blinded by the dazzling beam. Smith shielded his eyes, dived for the side of the roof, and snatched up a heavy iron boat-hook.

Mike recovered, and whirled to face him again. Smith hurled the boat-hook at him, and it smashed into the side of Graham's head. Mike staggered and fell to one knee,

then slumped to the floor. His knife flew from his hand,
skidded along the wet planks—and slipped over the edge
into the Seine.

The helicopter pilot waved at Smith, and made an urgent
motion of summons with his hand. From the side of the
machine, a winch-operated cable dropped to the wheelhouse roof and landed with a clang. Smith ran to it, and
dragged it down with him to the main deck of the bateau
mouche. He wrenched open the hatch-cover of a small
hold, and hooked the cable to a metal ring at the end of his
trio of ransom bags.

Smith pulled frantically on the rope, and the winch
brought the garish blue sausages up into the chopper's
belly.

Mike Graham started to come around, lurching painfully
to his feet, as the cable and hook descended once more.

Smith grabbed the hook with both hands, and yanked it
twice. He gave a fierce yell of exultation as he left the deck.

Graham's desperate shout followed Smith's on the wind.
Mike launched a furious charge that took him in one
jarring bound on to the deck below and, without pausing,
into a flying leap for Smith's trailing foot.

His hand grasped Smith's ankle, fingers digging into the
bone. The other hand came up and found the toe-cap of a
sensible brogue.

Smith hacked savagely with his free foot at Graham's
hands, crunching down on unprotected fingers time and
time again with shocking force.

Mike felt the flesh torn from his hands, and his last sen-
sation before he slipped despairingly into the river was the
snap of his little finger breaking.

Smith chanted "Come on! Faster! Faster!" as the helicopter zoomed away and he drew nearer to its welcoming
embrace.

Graham came up for the second time, and lashed the
water in ungovernable fury when he saw the man he hated
disappear into the chopper that would take him to freedom.

Smith clamped his hands on the landing skids, and pulled
himself into the chopper's hold. Other hands reached to
help him, to guide him safely away from the sliding door,
and to shut it behind him.

The exhausted man staggered across the helicopter and collapsed over his king's ransom for the hostage tower.

He rested his face on the wet, cold rubber, and tears of joy and relief started from his eyes. He pressed his lips to the blue bag, tasting its substance, smelling its brackish scent.

He had done it! He had won! The perfect crime, fashioned at the hands of the perfect criminal. The feeling that coursed through his body was almost orgasmic.

He was invincible! The Great Khan of crime, the most audacious adventurer in history!

No one could halt his relentless progress—nobody could stand against him. Not governments, nor agencies, nor armies. There was nothing—nothing—he could not achieve.

He was the indomitable, unconquerable criminal colossus of the world!

"Welcome aboard, Mister Smith," Malcolm Philpott said from the copilot's seat. "We've been expecting you."

Smith's head turned slowly in the direction of the voice. His eyes rested on the man who had spoken, and on the woman crouching beside him.

He panned along the whole length of the helicopter. Three grinning soldiers rocked on their heels in the swaying plane, machine guns pointed at his head and heart.

He sighed and looked back at the man in the copilot's seat.

Mister Smith smiled, fleetingly and resignedly, and said, "Touché, Mr. Philpott. Touché."

EPILOGUE

In a stunted butt-end of street between the Avenue Emile Deschamel and the Allée Adrienne Lecouvreur is a restaurant infinitely more salubrious than La Chatte Qui Siffle. On the day after Smith was taken into the unfriendly custody of the French police (and a traditionalist Examining Magistrate), Malcolm Philpott hosted a luncheon party for six—himself and Sonya Kolchinsky, C.W. and Sabrina, Mike Graham, and Commissioner Poupon.

On the way to the restaurant, Sonya had insisted on taking group photographs twice—against the backdrop of the middle pavilion dome at the École Militaire (where, as Poupon pointed out, Napoleon himself had been a cadet) and again by the equestrian statue of the Marne hero, Maréchal Joffre. They were in a mood to do full justice to a Lucullan meal, washed down with château wine at forty dollars a bottle.

Throughout the lunch, Philpott had deliberately kept the conversation light. He did not favor post mortems, and he was adept at steering the talk away from himself, Sonya, and UNACO. Philpott rightly considered that the less anyone knew about his organization—even his own agents—the better for the future of the department.

He was genuinely but shyly pleased to see a relationship growing between Graham and Sabrina. Mike's injured hands were still wrapped and bandaged, and Sabrina carefully cut the Châteaubriand she was sharing with him into manageable pieces, and even speared the odd segment of meat for him, greatly to his embarrassment.

C.W., seated next to Sabrina, amused himself by eavesdropping on Graham's attempts to persuade her to take a brief holiday with him in the south of France. Mike owned a hillside villa near Carcassonne, in Languedoc, and he spent a great deal of time extolling its virtues of beauty and solitude.

C.W. had observed the two of them easing naturally together on the tower. He knew a little of Graham's background, and much of Sabrina's, and he was not quite cynical enough not to hope that they'd make it.

"I'll think about it, Mike," Sabrina said. "I have a lot I want to do just at the moment, and I may take a raincheck on it . . . but really I would love to come."

"Nothing of these things you wish to do is of a criminal nature, I trust," Philpott teased.

"Why of course not, sir," she replied, fluttering her thick eyelashes at him. "How could you even suggest such a thing?"

"How indeed?" Philpott rejoined.

Graham coughed expertly to wean the subject away from crime. "There wouldn't, of course," he insisted, "be any strings. You'd be absolutely free to do anything you liked, with anyone you liked."

"Of course," she assented.

"Hon," C.W. leered, "if you believe that, you'd believe anything, as the Duke of Wellington said." Sabrina blushed, and Graham turned a look of mock fury on the sardonic black.

C.W. winked at him and said, "Only kidding, Mike. But it seemed to me from the way you described the place that there just wouldn't be anyone else within a hundred or so miles of it except good ole' Mike Graham. Huh?"

It was Philpott's turn to cough, not as expertly as Graham, but well enough. "Now I have a toast," he announced. "To all of us, for an operation well done. We may not have been on top all the time, but by God we sure caught up in the end."

They drank, and Philpott added, "And a special toast to you, Mike. It would have been impossible without you. You have our grateful thanks."

Mike flushed and said, "Aw, shucks," and Philpott got in quickly. "If you ever consider rejoining the Intelligence community, Mike, you might contact me. I think you'd find UNACO a little less, shall we say, orthodox than the CIA."

"Sure thing," C.W. supplemented, "unorthodox is the word. What do you say, Mike?"

Mike hesitated, and Sabrina laid her hand over his and said, "We did work well together, didn't we?"

Graham looked at each of the UNACO people in turn, his gaze resting longest on Sabrina. "Well," he replied slowly, "as someone once said to me when I invited her on an idyllic holiday in the south of France . . . I'll think about it."

Philpott beamed and said, "Any time, Mike. You'll be welcome any time." He then excused himself from the coffee and liqueurs. "There's something I have to do," he explained to Sonya. "It's a kind of tidying up. A few loose ends, you know. Just for the record—and your files. I'll see you back at the Ritz: and don't forget we're painting the Moulin Rouge red tonight."

"Think they'd mind a little black as well?" C.W. inquired innocently.

Lorenz van Beck had two hours to kill. But being a peaceable man, he decided to spend them more profitably.

This time he chose the Musée d'Art Moderne in the Avenue du President Wilson, and the Jeu de Paume in the Tuileries, Plâce de la Concorde, both for their superb modern French art. On reflection, he threw in the Centre Culturel Georges Pompidou, on the valid assumption that any construction of such an outré design would be unlikely to have provided for maximum security.

He rented a Peugeot estate car in the name of Maurice T. Randall—or so his British passport said—and drove to Rambouillet by a route so circuitous that it confounded him, let alone a possible tail.

Van Beck arrived at the church on the stroke of six o'clock, and poked his head around the door. The evening sun peeped weakly through the assembled stars and shepherds in the circular west window of sumptuously colored stained glass. There was enough light to see that he was alone, apart from a bald and shuffling sacristan, illogically moving sacred vessels from end to end of the altar at a commendably sluggish pace. Van Beck calculated he must be on overtime.

Van Beck tramped to the confessional boxes in his Church's shoes, that went rather well with the slim-fitting Savile Row suit and Jermyn Street shirt and tie. He was well-pleased with himself.

For good measure, and to make his day even more rewarding, he had visited the 14th-century Médici château at Rambouillet before keeping his ecclesiastical appointment. The château is nominally reserved for the President of the Republic, but van Beck didn't see how that automatically excluded him. Someone with talent, he thought, like—say—Sabrina Carver, could have a splendid time there. With or without the President.

The German drew back the stiff red curtain and sat on the penitent's seat. The figure behind the metal grille, head bowed, lips moving in silent prayer, said, "My son?"

"Bless me, Father, for I have sinned," van Beck mumbled.

"And how," Philpott replied. "For one thing, you've lied to me."

"I never lie," van Beck said matter-of-factly, "especially to clients."

"Then you didn't tell me the whole truth," Philpott persisted.

"Ah," Lorenz van Beck conceded, "that is an entirely different thing, Mr. Philpott. To which tactical omission are you referring?"

Philpott chuckled. "I like that, van Beck. Let me tell you then: when I debriefed Michael Graham, I was dismayed to learn that you had recommended not just Sabrina and C.W. to Smith, but Graham as well. Is that so?"

Van Beck admitted that it was. Philpott pondered the information. "Neither did you tell me," he went on, "that Graham had stolen the laser guns and handed them over to Smith—did you?"

That too, van Beck allowed, was true. "Nor that Smith had the lasers at his château in the Loire Valley," Philpott persisted.

"I had to leave you to find out something for yourself,"

the German complained, "and I had no possible doubt that with your Red priority enabling you to put a Lockheed SR 71 long-range reconnaissance plane into French air space, you would very quickly learn the location of Smith's little hideout. Which, after all, you did."

"True," Philpott said, disconcerted by van Beck's intimate knowledge of the "Blackbird" spy plane.

"I am given to understand," van Beck continued, "that this versatile aircraft can fly at a height of more than eighty thousand feet, and survey an area of sixty thousand square miles of territory in one hour. In addition to sophisticated radar and photographic equipment, it carries infrared sensors capable of detecting heat generated by the human body even when under cover. Is that not the case?"

"It is," said Philpott crossly.

"In effect," van Beck pressed on, "it could have taken an X-ray picture of Sabrina Carver in bed, which would indeed have been a notable achievement. Nein?"

"Ja," replied Philpott tersely, "and cut out the small talk. I want answers, and I want them now." The bald sacristan shuffled past the confessional boxes singing a Gregorian chant off-key.

Van Beck sighed heavily. "Very well, Mr. Philpott. I owe you that, at least. In any case, I was going to tell you." Philpott grunted, unconvinced.

"The first thing I would have you understand," van Beck began, "is that business is business. I work for whom I please, at any time I please. If I am employed by you and Smith simultaneously, I would be a fool to confess everything I learn to each of you. And I am not a fool, Mr. Philpott.

"The reason why I did not inform you about Graham is deeply personal," he went on. "I must have your assurance that what I am about to reveal will go no further." Philpott gave it.

Van Beck pursed his lips and coughed gently. "Did Graham tell you he had been hunting Smith because Smith was responsible for killing his wife?"

"Yes, he did. It was a dreadful story. I can appreciate that he had to leave the CIA to do that, although continuing to work for them unofficially, and under cover."

Van Beck nodded, and sighed again. "He didn't tell you the name of his wife, did he?" Philpott shook his head.

"But you do concede that Graham had good reason to go after Smith?"

"Of course," Philpott said, "any man would have done. He must have been half-crazed with grief."

Van Beck said, "He was."

Philpott looked sharply at him through the grille. "How do you know?" he demanded.

Van Beck said, "His wife's name was Sieglinde. He called her 'Ziggy.' She was twenty-five when she died. Before her marriage to Michael Graham, she was Anneliese Sieglinde van Beck.

"She was my only child, Mr. Philpott, and the unborn baby that was lost in her womb when Smith blew her to pieces would have been my grandchild."

Philpott was stunned, and kept silent. Van Beck held his head in his hands, and Philpott heard a stifled sob come from him.

"I'm sorry, Lorenz," he said gently, "I didn't know."

Van Beck sniffed and replied, "Of course not. How could you? But you see, Mr. Philpott, I had to make certain that Michael Graham—who is a fine young man—was the only weapons expert infiltrated into Smith's organization.

"And once I had done that, I resolved to do nothing to put his cover at risk. The CIA had hushed up the story of his wife's death, making it seem natural causes. It isn't even on his file. They fabricated a mental breakdown, and released him for the one purpose of taking Smith. I do not work for the CIA, Mr. Philpott, but I would gladly do again what I did to revenge myself on a monster like Smith."

Philpott replied, "I see that now. And of course you acted rightly."

"In other ways, too, Mr. Phlipott," van Beck went on. "Tell me, who gave you the tipoff that Smith was planning another big job?"

"As far as I was concerned, INTERPOL."

"And who told INTERPOL—under a veil of secrecy, and on condition that they passed the intelligence to you?"

Philpott smiled. "Obviously, you did." Van Beck nodded. "I believed the CIA or INTERPOL would bungle the job," he whispered, "and I was confident that UNACO would not."

Philpott said wryly, "Thanks for that, anyway. OK, van Beck, that's cleared the air. I hope our association will be as fruitful in the future as it has been in the past."

Van Beck grunted and rose from his chair. "Then I may go?" Philpott nodded; but held up a hand as the German made to leave.

"There's just one thing," he said. "It's fairly important. What happened," he asked carefully, "to the proceeds of Sabrina's admirably executed robbery in the Amsterdam Diamond Exchange, for which I imagine you were also responsible?"

Van Beck smiled a crooked smile. "The diamonds were passed on to me, and I have already disposed of them. Miss Carver has been paid, and I shall consider my commission a suitable reward for information leading to the return of four extremely dangerous and secret laser guns. No? Business, after all, as I keep telling you, Mr. Philpott, is always business."

Philpott chuckled, and said, "You win, then. Auf wiedersehen, Lorenz."

"Goodbye," van Beck replied. "Until the next time."

Philpott heard the church door slam behind him, then got to his feet and made his own way out, pausing to bestow a blessing on the sacristan. He took off his priestly vestments and hung them on the cloakroom peg where he had found them.

He passed through the porch and out into the balmy twilight. The air was good. He filled his lungs and stretched.

Yes, he thought, the next time. With Sonya, Sabrina, and C.W. on his team—and, possibly, Mike Graham too—Philpott was keenly looking forward to whatever might come UNACO's way.

Who, though, would it be the next time? It was a comforting problem to take with him back to the Ritz.